D0965719

# TWO STRIKES

# TWO STRIKES
## Johnny Boateng

**James Lorimer & Company Ltd., Publishers**
**Toronto**

Copyright © by Johnny Boateng
First published in Canada in 2016.
First published in the United States in 2017.

All rights reserved. No part of this book may be reproduced or transmitted
in any form or by any means, electronic or mechanical, including photo-
copying, or by any information storage or retrieval system, without permis-
sion in writing from the publisher.

James Lorimer & Company Ltd., Publishers acknowledges the support of
the Ontario Arts Council (OAC), an agency of the Government of Ontario,
which in 2015-16 funded 1,676 individual artists and 1,125 organiza-
tions in 209 communities across Ontario for a total of $50.5 million. We
acknowledge the support of the Canada Council for the Arts, which last year
invested $153 million to bring the arts to Canadians throughout the country.
This project has been made possible in part by the Government of Canada
and with the support of the Ontario Media Development Corporation.

978-1-4594-1150-0
eBook also available 978-1-4594-1148-7

Cataloguing data available from Library and Archives Canada.

Published by:
James Lorimer &
Company Ltd., Publishers
117 Peter Street,
Suite 304
Toronto, ON, Canada
M5V 0M3
www.lorimer.ca

Distributed by:
Lerner Publishing Services
1251 Washington Ave N
Minneapolis, MN, USA
55401
www.lernerbooks.com

Printed and bound in Canada.
Manufactured by Friesens Corporation in Altona, Manitoba, Canada in
December 2016.
Job #228985

*In loving memory of Izell Scotland*

*A special thank you to my coaches and teachers, Terry Jones, John Ritchie, Wayne Naka, Brent and Joel Tremblay, Carlo Mason and Brian Baldwin, Coach Pepe, Tim and Bernie Mcmahon. I will always cherish you and all of the wonderful people in the home of champions. Thank you.*

# CONTENTS

# PROLOGUE:
# WARM-UP

*Crank!* A well-hit baseball screamed through the crisp spring air. It soared over a green chain-link fence in centre field and disappeared into the forest surrounding the park.

*Crack!* The baseball smashed into tree branches somewhere deep in the woods.

KaLeah Watson stood at home plate with her wooden bat in her hands. She twirled the bat and leaned on it like it was a cane.

"I got all of that one. Eh, Dad?" Kal said.

Kal's dad stared out into centre field. He shook his head and wiped the sweat from his forehead. Kal could see that his cheeks were turning bright red.

"You sure did. Great job of keeping your weight back and busting your hips."

Kal looked at the bat in her hands.

"I think I broke the bat, Dad."

Kal's dad made his way to the batter's box and took the bat from Kal's hands. "Yup, she's done. Cracked her right down the middle," he said.

"Aw, man. I loved that bat," Kal said.

"Yeah, she was a beauty. Well, it's getting late. Let's head home."

"C'mon, Dad, we just got here. I'll grab Trapper," Kal said, reaching for her baseball glove, "and you can throw me some pitches."

"Honey, I'm tired and sunburned. My arm is killing me. And I have to get to work. I'm running late for my patrol." Kal's dad was an RCMP officer, and the only family Kal had left.

"Mom would've stayed, even when she was sick. And she would have thrown harder than you," Kal said.

He chuckled. "Your mother did have one heck of an arm. But you get your hitting from me. You know your old man was a stud! How do you think I snagged your mother?"

"Sure, Dad." Remembering her mom, Kal suddenly grew quiet.

Her dad placed his arm around Kal. "She'd be very proud of you," he said.

Kal managed a smile. She watched her dad head home.

*Squeak!* The gate to the field swung open. A red-headed boy holding a bucket of baseballs walked onto the field. He wore a black baseball cap with TRAIL ALL-STARS on it.

As Kal watched, the boy started a routine of warm-up stretching. He turned and stared back at Kal.

"Hey," the boy said.

"Hey," Kal replied nervously.

"Haven't seen you here before."

"I just moved to Trail from Halifax."

"That's cool. I'm Joey. What's your name?"

"Don't be too late, KaLeah," her dad called back over his shoulder.

"Is that your old man, KaLeah?" Joey asked.

"It's *Kal*," she said. "Why do you ask?"

"Oh, I just thought . . . because he's . . . well, you're . . ." Joey stammered.

"I'm just messing with you, Joey. My mom was black."

"Got it. Your dad is leaving you here?"

"He's gotta go to work. He works for the RCMP."

The boy walked over to the pitching mound and picked up Kal's baseball glove.

"This thing is a beauty. Sure looks like it's seen a lot of baseball. Is this yours?"

"Yeah, well, it was my dad's old catcher's mitt, but it's mine now."

"*You* can backcatch?" Joey said, laughing.

Kal snatched her glove from Joey. "Of course I can."

Joey's smile faded. "You think you could catch me?"

"Why not?"

"Look, the guys in my grade can't handle my stuff. Even tenth graders have a hard time. I throw pure gas."

"Gas?" Kal said.

"Yeah, gas, you know — lasers."

"That's dumb." Kal giggled to herself over the way Joey was bragging.

"You think you can catch me? I don't think you should try."

Kal placed her glove on her hand. "Are you going to talk all day, or what?"

Joey smiled. "Your old man's a cop. I don't want him to arrest me if you go home crying or something."

"Bring it!" Kal yelled. She punched her baseball glove and pushed her curly hair back from her face.

# 1 TOP OF THE FIRST INNING: TOUGH AS NAILS

The brown glove Kal had on was worn. But she loved the way it felt in her hand. She loved the way it smelled like raw leather and dirt and a little like old sweat. Kal traced her fingers over the stitching that spelled TRAPPER on the side of the glove. With Trapper in her hand, Kal felt like she could catch anything.

"Kal, you're new, so I'm telling you straight up. You can't handle my stuff. No seventh grader can," Joey said.

"I'm in grade eight, and I got this!" Kal called out as she settled into a crouch.

"When I'm in the Major Leagues, you'll be able to say you played catch with me."

"I can probably spit harder than you throw," Kal shouted.

"Oh ya?" Joey laughed. He seemed to enjoy Kal's trash-talking. "Just remember, you asked for it."

Kal could barely see Joey's eyes behind the shadow cast by his baseball cap. But she knew he was locked in on hitting Trapper with everything he had.

Kal pounded Trapper with her fist and held out her hand as a target.

Joey wound up and delivered the pitch.

The red seams that wrapped around the ball hissed through the crisp air like a snake. The pitch was high, hard and a little to the left. It was coming so fast, Kal could barely see the ball. Without thinking, she caught the ball.

SSMACK! The ball hit with so much speed and power it almost took Kal's glove off. Kal couldn't hang on to it, and dropped it out of her glove.

There wasn't much padding in Trapper. Kal felt the sting of Joey's fastball and her hand began to throb. It really hurt, but she'd never let Joey know it.

"Wow! Nice heater!" Kal yelled. She scooped the ball up with her glove and flicked it neatly into her right hand.

"Seriously!? I can't believe you snagged that one. I don't think I've ever thrown that hard to a girl," Joey said.

Kal threw the ball with a little extra speed back to Joey. She wanted to let him know she had a strong arm, too.

Joey casually snagged the ball out of the air.

"Maybe it was luck," Joey said.

"Maybe," Kal said. "Throw another one." Her hand was numb. Joey's fastball scared her a little.

But she loved it.

"How fast do you throw, Joey?" Kal asked.

"I've been clocked by scouts at almost 90 miles per hour," Joey said.

"Okay," Kal said.

Joey frowned a little. "They were pro scouts," he said.

"Okay," Kal said.

"As in the show? Do you know what that is?"

"Yeah, the Major Leagues. I get it."

"You're not impressed?"

"Well, not really."

"Why not?" Joey demanded.

Kal quickly backtracked. She didn't want to offend the first person she had met in this town. Especially one she could play baseball with.

"I'm just kidding. I think it's pretty awesome," Kal said. *Why would he care what she thought, anyway?*

Joey threw Kal a few more fastballs and she caught them all. Kal was starting to get the hang of catching the ball in the webbing of the glove. The last one didn't even hurt.

"Let's see how you handle my curveball, Kal," Joey shouted.

Joey wiped the sweat from his brow as he walked back to the mound. He cleared his throat and spat dark gobs of gooey saliva everywhere.

"Gross!" Kal muttered.

"What? It's just chewing tobacco. Girls dig it," Joey said.

"I doubt it." Kal couldn't see how any girl would find that attractive.

Joey spat out the tobacco. "Happy?"

Kal shrugged her shoulders.

"Okay, see if you can keep *this* bender in front of you, *Kal*," Joey said.

Kal crouched down. With her hand, she brushed curly strands of hair out of her tanned face and twisted her ball cap backward.

"I'm ready!" Kal snapped back.

Kal's legs tensed. She popped up on her toes as Joey wound up. The ball rocketed from Joey's right arm. It curved sharply and nose-dived to the ground a few feet in front of Kal.

She wasn't sure if she could snag it. So Kal drove her left foot into the ground and slid to her right to get her body in front of the ball.

The ball bounced sharply off the ground and hit Kal square in the nose. Her eyes welled up with tears. She had never been hit in the face with the ball before. It hurt a lot.

"Oh, snap. You okay?" Joey asked as he approached Kal.

Through the pain, a toothy grin crossed Kal's face. The baseball was spinning like a top in front of her. Kal scooped up the ball.

"How's that for a block! You like that, Joey?" Kal yelled.

"Damn, Kal. That was sick. Mad respect. But your faced is real messed up. Please don't tell your old man on me; he'll lock me up or something."

"I won't tell," Kal promised.

"You're tough as nails, Kal. Let's do this again sometime," Joey said.

"Sure!" Kal said as she cupped her hand over her face. Bright red drops of blood dripped onto her hand. She pinched her nose to stop the bleeding.

As soon as she got home, she rushed into the bathroom and peered into the mirror.

"Wow." She was glad her Dad was at work.

Was her nose broken?

Tomorrow was supposed to be her first day at her new school.

Kal stared at the blood on her face and the huge bump forming on her nose.

"Great. Just great."

# 2 BOTTOM OF THE FIRST INNING: HOME OF CHAMPIONS

Kal waited for the bus listening to some hip hop music she had downloaded on her phone. With no one around, Kal felt comfortable working on her dance moves. She twirled and *dabbed* as the music blasted in her ears. Kal knew all the latest steps, but *dabbing* had become her favourite. Kal danced some more. A car rolled past and an old white lady gave her strange look. Embarrassed, Kal removed her headphones. She checked the time. She'd been waiting for twenty minutes. How could she have missed the bus?

She decided to walk to school. As she walked up the steep hill leading to Riverview Middle School, she turned around and saw the bus roll past the spot she'd just left.

*Already bad luck*, Kal thought to herself.

Kal had been dreading this first day at a new school. She would stand out, with her dark skin and hair so kinky and so hard to deal with that Kal had just let it grow into a wild golden afro. As far as Kal knew, there wasn't another black person in all of Trail.

Today, she'd also be the new girl with a silly cartoon bandage across the bridge of her bruised nose.

Through a clearing in the trees, Kal could see the entire town. It was a pretty town, with a large river and some bridges. She still missed Halifax. She missed the big city. In her old neighbourhood, there were many families of mixed backgrounds and colours, like hers. There, it was white kids who stood out.

As Kal continued up the mountain path, she wound her way around a steep rock cliff. She picked up stones and hurled them at various targets.

*Ping!* Kal hit a rusty old can.

*Thud!* A maple tree at least 20 metres away.

*Thwack!* Her rock smashed into a dead tree stump about 35 metres away. Pieces of wood exploded into the air like fireworks.

"Bull's eye!" Kal whispered.

Kal picked up a stick and a round stone. She tossed the stone into the air and swung the stick smoothly and quickly.

*Crack!* The stone soared down the mountainside and disappeared into the trees. *Home run!*

Kal jogged up the mountainside.

As she jogged along the path, rays of sun splashed her slightly freckled face. Large mountain peaks cast their shadows over the town in the valley. The raging Columbia River twisted and wound its way under gigantic metallic bridges that separated East Trail from

West Trail. Kal looked nervously at the raging rapids and whirlpools. She missed the sounds of seagulls and the smell of the ocean.

The small town sprawled out on both sides of the valley. Looking around in each direction, Kal couldn't see past the mountains. She was surrounded, trapped in Trail.

*Click! Clack! Click! Clack!*

A sound like firecrackers echoed through the trees.

Kal wiped the sweat from her brow and slowed her pace.

*Click! Clack!* The sound grew louder.

Kal recognized the sound. It was the sound of baseball cleats.

Like an army, several boys wearing black baseball caps jogged past in single file. Kal crept close behind.

Kal could hear them laughing and joking around. Some of them looked to be her age and some were older. They jogged past a monument and a sign that read HOME OF CHAMPIONS and each boy tapped it with his glove.

Kal checked the time on her phone. It was only 7:30 a.m. and these boys were training.

The procession of boys marched onward toward a place that looked like some giant had taken a huge spoon and carved a ballpark into the mountainside. Kal followed, staying out of sight.

★★★

The park was a beautiful shade of green. It looked like each blade of grass in the infield had been clipped with a pair of scissors. The boys took their positions in the field.

"Okay, Trail Boys. Bases loaded. Ghost infield," shouted a voice. It came from a slender man wearing a uniform that looked way too big for him. He stood at the plate with a bat, but no baseball. All the players crouched down in ready positions.

The coach threw an invisible ball into the air and pretended to bunt it.

The third baseman charged toward home plate. The backcatcher flipped off his mask and charged toward third base.

"I got it," yelled the backcatcher. He pretended to field the imaginary baseball with his bare hand. He pretended to throw the ball to first base.

The first baseman looked at the invisible ball in the dirt. He did the splits to lean forward and scoop it up. He quickly fired the ball back to home plate. The backcatcher stood behind home plate and caught the ball. He then fell backward, as if an invisible runner had steamrolled into him. Kal could almost see it. It looked so real.

The catcher fell onto his back and held the baseball in the air. He'd survived the hit, and hung onto the ball.

"Double play," Kal whispered under her breath. The boys continued to play against their ghost infield as Kal watched in amazement. She could almost see the baseball, even though there wasn't one. She could imagine the baserunners, even though there weren't any.

The ghost infield was coolest thing Kal had ever seen.

Even from a distance, Kal could hear the laughter coming from the field. Those Trail Boys seemed to be having so much fun, like they were one big group of friends. *Friends.*

The thought of her old teammates in Halifax brought Kal back to where she was. She was a new kid in a town that was really serious about baseball.

Kal reached into her backpack and pulled out Trapper. *Would they let her play?*

Kal slid Trapper back into her pack and zipped up. She swung her bag over her shoulder and took off running.

# 3 TOP OF THE SECOND INNING: NEW GIRL

*Smush! Smush!* Kal sprinted through the dew-soaked grass in front of the middle school. A heavy man with small glasses and a bushy moustache was standing in the middle of the field. He held a large ball bag full of bats and softballs. He looked at Kal, then at his clipboard and then at his wristwatch.

"Just made it. You must be the new girl, KaLeah, right?"

"It's Kal."

"You're pretty tall, Kal; do you play basketball?"

Kal looked down at him. It was bad enough standing out for being tall without people mentioning it.

"A little," Kal said.

"Well, Kal, I'm Mr. Sims, your PE teacher. We're playing softball today. How about you go ahead and join your team in the field. You know how to play, right?"

Kal nodded. She jogged onto the field holding Trapper under her arm. Everyone stared at her as she took her position at shortstop.

Kal felt a tap on her shoulder. She turned to see an Asian girl with long, dark hair and a smile in her face.

"I've got third base," the girl said.

Kal nodded.

"I've never seen you before. What's your name?" the girl asked.

"Kal."

"Cool. Nice to meet you, Kal. I'm Sarah Chong," she said. "So, what are you?"

"Excuse me?" Who asks something like that? Kal wondered.

"What are you? Like Spanish or mulatto or something?" Sarah smiled.

"My dad is white and my mom was black," Kal said.

"Your mom was black? You mean she isn't anymore?" Sarah smiled.

"No, I mean, she's . . . Never mind, I'm mixed."

"Oh, okay, well you have awesome hair, Kal. I wish I had hair like that."

Kal managed a smile. *No, you don't*, Kal thought.

Three girls on the other team were wearing matching green and white softball team hats, shorts and black knee-high socks. *Who does that for gym class?* Kal thought.

"Hey, Kal, if you're going to play shortstop, how about you grab an infielder's glove from the bag instead of using that old catcher's mitt," Mr. Sims said.

Kal looked at the gloves in the bag. They looked more worn than Trapper.

"That's okay. I'm good with this one."

The three girls in matching outfits laughed at Kal's response.

Kal frowned. *Who were those girls?*

As if she read her thoughts, Sarah Chong whispered, "That's Nikki Collins, Marcy Osmond and Jenny Cooper. Be ready, they can hit."

Mr. Sims took the mound. Marcy stepped up to the plate. She swung at the first pitch Mr. Sims threw.

*Crack!* The ball skipped through the grass to Kal's right. Kal scooped the ball up effortlessly. She leaped into the air and threw a perfect strike to first base to throw Marcy out.

"You're out, Marcy! Nice play, Kal!" Mr. Sims yelled.

"Nice one, Kal!" Sarah yelled.

Marcy glared at Kal as she jogged back to the dugout. Kal saw Marcy whisper something in Nikki's ear.

Nikki eyed Kal with a mean look on her face.

Jenny was next up to the plate. She also swung at the first pitch.

*Crack!*

"That's it, Jenny!" Marcy hollered.

Jenny hit the ball hard, but it was right at Kal. The ball dipped in the air and bounced right in front of her. Kal calmly snagged the ball out of the air. She took one step and threw the ball sidearm to first base. The throw was well ahead of Jenny, even though she'd been hustling to beat the throw.

"You're out!" Mr. Sims yelled. "Nice snag, Kal!" he added.

Kal smiled and nodded her head.

A hush spread across the field. Kal heard some of the boys laughing. It didn't sound like they were laughing at her.

Nikki Collins stepped to the plate with her blond ponytail bouncing behind her. She glared at Kal and tapped the plate aggressively with her bat.

On the first pitch, Nikki grunted and swung so hard that she nearly fell over. She missed the pitch badly.

Kal muffled her laugh, but Nikki saw it.

*Clank!* Nikki tapped the plate even harder with her bat.

"You can do better than that pitch, Mr. Sims!" Nikki snapped.

"Okay, Nikki, here it comes," he said.

Kal dug in at shortstop and leaned forward on her toes.

As the pitch came in, Nikki kicked out her leg and swung even harder.

*Crack!* She'd hit the ball dead on. It was a line drive right up the middle of the field. Mr. Sims's baseball cap went flying into the air as he ducked out of the way. The ball had nearly taken his head off.

From the moment the ball was hit, Kal was on the move. She ranged with cat-like quickness to her left. Kal dove, her body fully extended. She plucked the ball out of mid-air.

The girls in the field cheered like their team had just won the World Series. Sarah Chong ran over from third base and hugged Kal.

"That was awesome!" Sarah shrieked.

Nikki Collins stood at home plate, her hands on her hips and a scowl on her face.

Kal's team was at bat. When it was her turn, she picked the heaviest aluminum bat she could find. Mr. Sims was throwing the ball underhand and Kal wanted to make sure she didn't get ahead of the pitch.

Kal stepped into the batter's box.

"Easy out!" Nikki shouted.

Kal ignored Nikki. It was clear the girl had a problem with her, but Kal couldn't figure out what it was.

"Ready, Kal?" Mr. Sims called.

Kal nodded. How ready did she need to be for an underhand pitch?

Kal looked out into centre field. A lanky boy with long, blond hair stood there in an athletic stance. Kal recognized the black baseball cap he wore. It was like the one Joey wore and the ones the Trail Boys were wearing.

Kal looked out into left field. Two girls were sitting in the grass, barely paying attention to the game. *Perfect.*

The pitch came in so slow, Kal felt like it was taking forever to reach the plate. Kal was used to hitting baseballs, so the big softball looked like a watermelon coming toward her.

Kal kept her eye on the ball and swung smoothly.

*Crack!* The ball rocketed into the sky deep into left field.

"Wow, Kal, you're a natural!" Mr. Sims shouted.

Kal looked up to see how far the ball was going.

The girls in left field screamed, thinking the ball was going to hit them.

Kal began her home run jog to first base.

"I got it!"

Kal looked up to see a boy sprinting with blistering speed into left field. His black hat flew off as he ran, and his blond hair flapped behind him.

The boy dove, his body fully extended, and caught the ball.

Kal was amazed. It was the same boy who had been standing in centre field.

"Nice catch, DeeJay!" Nikki shouted.

Kal waited at second base as the boy ran up to her.

"Nice hit," he said.

"Nice catch," Kal answered.

# 4 BOTTOM OF THE SECOND INNING: FOUL PLAY

Kal sat in the back of Social Studies class daydreaming. She twiddled her pen through her fingers like a teeter-totter.

When the bell rang to end the day, Kal gathered her books and headed to her locker. The Trail middle school only went up to the eighth grade so she was a senior. In Halifax, Kal would have a year away from being a senior in junior high school. It felt different being among the oldest in the school. Most of the younger kids stared at her and made weird and curious faces as she walked through the hallway.

All of the other kids were in pairs or groups. Everyone in the school seemed to have friends, except her.

"Wait up, Kal!" Sarah shouted as she ran down the hall.

Sarah followed Kal to her locker. "You're an awesome ball player," she said. "Where did you learn how to play?"

"Watching TV. And my dad taught me," Kal said.

"You sure showed up the Valley Girls," Sarah said.

"Valley Girls?" Kal asked.

"Yeah — Nikki, Marcy and Jenny. They play for the Valley all-star softball team, and they're probably the best players in the school. But you sure showed them up today."

Kal didn't know what all the fuss was about. It was just a game in gym class.

"Here they come," Sarah whispered.

A group of seventh grade girls laughed and joked with each other as they walked to their lockers. As they crossed in front of the Valley Girls, they bumped into Nikki slightly. The older girl stopped in her tracks.

"Excuse you?" Nikki shouted.

The younger girls looked horrified.

"Watch it!" Marcy snapped.

"Don't you seventh-grade losers ever cut us off again. Got that?" Nikki said.

"Sorry, Nikki," they whispered.

"Don't even look at me, you little bitches," Nikki said.

"Seriously, not cool," Marcy added.

"Yeah, no kidding," Jenny chimed in.

The Valley Girls stormed past the group of seventh graders and marched toward Kal and Sarah.

"Nik, did you see the look on their faces?" Marcy giggled.

"Yeah, I love being a senior," Nikki said.

Nikki, Marcy and Jenny surrounded Kal.

Nikki was chomping her gum like a cow chewing its cud. She glared at Kal with a wicked smile on her pretty face.

"What?" Kal snapped.

"You're a show-off, you know that?" Nikki said.

"Whatever," Kal said. She tried to step around the three girls, but Nikki blocked her path.

Marcy and Jenny giggled. Nikki kept her eyes locked on Kal.

"I bet you think you were pretty hot stuff today in gym class, hey?" Nikki said, crossing her arms.

Kal shrugged her shoulders. "No big deal. It's just gym softball. It's not that hard," Kal said dryly.

Nikki curled her lip, ready to respond, when a boy's voice rang out.

"Make-over, Collins!"

A large, dirty hand gripped the top of Nikki's head and ruffled her hair.

Nikki shrieked. She whipped around to see who dared to touch her.

A stocky boy with a black Trail All-Stars cap stood smiling behind her. Beside him, a smaller, skinny boy with braces was grinning ear-to-ear.

"Brody Mccarthy!" Nikki shouted.

"Face wash!" he shouted. He put his grimy hands in Marcy's and Jenny's faces.

"Ew!" they shouted.

"Get lost, Brody!" Nikki took a swing at Brody. But he dodged it and took off down the hall.

Kal couldn't help but smirk.

"What's so funny, Jungle Book? Nice cartoon Band-Aid and nice nose," said Nikki, turning on Kal.

"Look at her monkey nose," Marcy whispered as she cupped her mouth in laughter.

"Are you covering up a zit or something?" Jenny added.

"If she is, she missed a spot, and another one, and another one, oh look, there's another one," Marcy teased.

"Give her a break," Sarah pleaded.

"Shut up, Sarah," Marcy snapped.

"Come on, girls, let's leave guppy lips here alone," Nikki joked.

Jenny and Marcy giggled some more.

Her heart pounding in her chest, Kal clenched her fist.

Kal pushed passed the girls and walked briskly down the hallway. No one had ever said things like that to her before. Worse yet, Kal didn't know what she had done to deserve it.

As she walked down the hall, her fist was still clenched and tears welled in her eyes.

★★★

Kal boarded a yellow school bus packed with kids chattering, fooling around and gossiping. Kal made her way to an empty seat at the back of the bus. Marcy, Jenny and Nikki boarded the bus and squeezed into one seat close to the front.

Sarah walked up the aisle after Marcy, Jenny and Nikki. They waved *too bad* to Sarah and laughed in her face. Dejected, Sarah made her way to the back of the bus and sat down beside Kal.

Marcy, Jenny and Nikki looked back and glared right at Kal. Then they pointed and laughed.

"Don't mind them," Sarah whispered.

Suddenly everyone on the bus started shouting.

"Food fight!" a voice yelled from the front of the bus.

Sarah grabbed Kal by the arm and pulled her down behind the seat. "Get down!" she shrieked.

*Splat!* Half of a banana smashed against the back window just above Sarah's head.

Everyone was hurling food all over the bus.

Sarah's eyes lit up. "You should totally join our soft-ball team, Kal!" Sarah's face beamed with excitement. "Marcy, Nikki and Jenny play, too. My mom could totally pick you up for practice."

"I don't know," Kal said.

"C'mon, just come out to one practice. Where do you live?"

Kal hesitated. She didn't really want to go to

practice. But Sarah was the only friendly face she had seen at school.

"I'll text you my address," Kal said.

"Sweet! I'll pick you up on Tuesday morning," Sarah said.

Kal popped her head up above the seat, then had to duck to barely avoid a celery stick whizzing past her head. The celery bounced off the back of the bus window and fell into Kal's hair.

The celery stick was covered with cream cheese and raisins. The cream cheese knotted in her curls. Kal picked the celery out of her hair and tossed it into the aisle. *Gross.*

Kal stood up and looked around. Nikki, Marcy and Jenny huddled together snickering. One of them must have thrown it.

"You'll love being on our team! Trust me," Sarah said.

Kal looked at Sarah's smiling face. Was Sarah too nice to realize when other people were being mean to her? How could she be friends with the Valley Girls?

While Sarah went on about how fun softball was, Kal fumed with anger. She rummaged through her backpack and found a half-eaten container of chocolate pudding.

Before she could think twice, her right arm wound back and the pudding flew. It careened wildly across the bus, right toward the Valley Girls.

*Splat!* The pudding container bounced off the window, splattering pudding all over Nikki, Marcy and Jenny. They shrieked loudly.

"Who the heck threw that!?" Marcy stood up with her hands on her hips.

"Wow!" Sarah said with a concerned look on her face. "I can't believe you just did that."

The other students on the bus cheered and threw more food.

Kal ducked behind the seat. She couldn't believe she'd done it either. She wasn't sure if she had meant to hit them or just scare them, but the damage was done.

The bus grinded to halt. Marcy, Jenny, Nikki and Sarah all got off at the same stop. As they stormed off the bus, Nikki gave Kal the middle finger.

Sarah followed after them and quickly waved. She mouthed "bye" to Kal.

The school bus slowed as it neared Kal's house. Kal picked up her backpack, brushed cookie crumbs off her shoulder and proceeded to the exit. As she walked, raisins fell out of her hair.

As the bus rolled to a stop, Kal smiled at the bus driver, who didn't look at all impressed. The front of the bus was littered with cookies, half-eaten fruit and raw vegetables. The bus driver's bushy grey eyebrows were furrowed in a frown as she tried to brush yogurt off her pant leg. She still managed a smile and wave as Kal jumped off the bus.

As the bus pulled away, Kal walked along the streets of East Trail, thinking about her day.

"Heads-up!" a voice yelled.

Kal looked up. A round brownish object was falling directly toward her. She didn't panic. She cupped her hands over her face and caught it.

Kal stared at the baseball in her hand. She removed Trapper from her backpack and walked over to the ballpark across the street.

# 5 TOP OF THE THIRD INNING: TRAIL BOYS

Dead patches of grass made the field look like a checkerboard. The field was filled with boys with gloves. The Trail Boys. Kal could hear them using coarse language and could see them play-fighting in the field.

As soon as Kal entered the field, they all paused to look at her. The biggest kid in the group stepped forward.

Kal recognized him as the one who had embarrassed the Valley Girls at school.

"She has our freakin' ball, Brody!" one of the boys yelled.

Brody Mccarthy approached Kal. He had a stubby build, a chubby face and he wore his cap backward.

"Give us our frickin' ball back," Brody said.

"Tell her B-Mac," some boys shouted from the field.

Building up her nerve, Kal flicked the worn-out baseball to him.

"Can I try a couple?" she asked. She set her backpack down in the grass.

"You're joking, right? Why don't you go play boob ball with your Valley Girls," Brody smirked.

The boys in the field burst into laughter. A kid at third base keeled over in hysterics.

The skinny kid with braces and a black ball cap worn so low it covered his eyes ran up beside Brody, snickering.

"You really think you can play with us?" he said to Kal, spitting through his braces on the ground in front of her. He kept spitting like he'd swallowed a fly.

"I do," Kal said, though she wasn't totally sure.

The tall, blond boy from gym class jogged in from the field.

"Give her a shot, Brody," he said, staring at Kal.

Brody pulled out a pouch of Big League Chew gum from his pocket and filled the other side of his mouth.

"No freakin' way, DeeJay." He turned to Kal and spat a blue gob at her feet. "Go home. We're in the middle of a freakin' derby."

*Was everyone always so tough in Trail? Or was that just the way they talked?* Kal wondered. She thought about grabbing her backpack and going home. But before she could finish her thought, her mouth was already forming the words.

"What's the matter? Scared I can hit it farther than you?"

Kal couldn't believe she'd actually said that. Her stomach churned and her legs shook, but she held her ground. She was taller than Brody and it seemed to bother him that he had to look up to talk to her.

The boys in the field stopped laughing and joking around. Like a pack of wolves, they raced into the field and surrounded Brody and Kal.

An angry look crept across Brody's dirty face.

"Nobody hits it farther than me," Brody said. "Who led in homers last season, Rocco?" He crossed his arms.

The skinny boy looked at Brody, but then he looked at DeeJay.

"I did!" DeeJay shouted at Brody before Rocco could answer.

Kal looked nervously at the boys around her.

"That's just in house league! I had you beat where it counts, in all-star play," Brody shouted back.

"That's only because I bat ahead of you and no one wants to pitch to me. You see nothing but fastballs, Brody!" DeeJay said.

"Oh, here he goes again, whining. You only bat there because your dad is the coach! Hey, DeeJay, are you going to cry again to Coach Daddy? Huh, DeeJay? Huh, sissy boy? We all know that's what you do whenever you don't get your way," he taunted.

DeeJay shoved Brody hard in the chest.

Rocco jumped in front of Brody. A few of the other Trail Boys grabbed DeeJay.

Kal felt a tingle of fear.

"Anytime, Brody! Anytime!" DeeJay shouted.

"I'm right here!" Brody shouted back.

"Well, she's the one calling you out, Brody. You afraid to go against her?" DeeJay said.

Brody shook Rocco off and squared up to DeeJay.

"Everyone here heard it! So are you taking her challenge or are you too chicken?" DeeJay said, not backing down.

All the boys in the park, including Rocco, turned to Brody.

Brody turned to Kal. "You want a piece of me? Fine. Me and Rocco stick. DeeJay, you can go with your girlfriend."

A cheer went out from the boys in the field. The boys forming the circle ran out excitedly to join them. They were arguing about who was going to win.

DeeJay walked up to Kal.

"It's you and me versus them," DeeJay said.

"What do you mean? Versus who?" Kal asked.

"We're a team. I pitch to Brody, you backcatch. Then you pitch to Rocco and I catch. Then it's our turn at bat. Whichever team has the most home runs after that wins the derby. Got it?"

"Got it," Kal said. She felt a rush of excitement.

"You've played baseball before, right? Not just softball?" DeeJay asked.

"Yeah. Of course."

"Just hit like you did in PE class, and I'll do the rest," DeeJay said.

Rocco and Brody were huddled up and going over their game plan.

DeeJay turned to Kal.

"We need to kick their butts," DeeJay said.

Kal nodded.

"We'll pitch first," DeeJay shouted.

"Fine!" Brody shouted back.

"What pitches can you throw?" Kal asked.

DeeJay seemed surprised by the question. "I have a slider, a curveball and my fastball."

"Okay, I'll put down one finger for the heater, two for the curve and three for the slider," Kal said.

"Uh, just don't call the slider too much."

Kal nodded. It was good to know which pitches DeeJay was more confident in. Kal grabbed Trapper and crouched down behind the plate.

"Three outs each," Rocco shouted.

# 6 BOTTOM OF THE THIRD INNING: DERBY

Brody stepped into the batter's box.

Kal called for the fastball. DeeJay wound up and delivered the pitch.

Brody swung and hit a ground ball. It went off to the right side of the infield.

"Dammit!" Brody shouted.

"Foul. That's an out," DeeJay shouted.

Kal called for the fastball again. DeeJay shook his head.

Kal called for the curveball. DeeJay nodded and threw.

Brody swung hard.

*CRACK!* The ball flew off his bat and sailed over the wooden fence in left field. Kal didn't quite see where or when it landed.

The boys in the field screamed and cheered.

Kal tried to hide how impressed she was. Brody had absolutely crushed DeeJay's pitch.

"Homer! 1–0," Rocco yelled.

Brody smiled at Kal. "See. That was a bomb!" he whispered.

Kal called for fastball. This time DeeJay nodded.

DeeJay wound up and delivered the pitch.

Brody swung and hit a line drive toward shortstop. One of the Trail Boys in the field dove and caught it.

"Two out!" DeeJay shouted.

Kal called for the curveball. DeeJay shook his head.

Kal slapped her glove and called for the curveball again. This time DeeJay agreed and delivered the pitch.

Brody swung so hard that he lost his balance, and then stumbled.

The ball shot off his bat and straight up into the air.

Kal stood up.

"Mine!" Kal shouted. She caught the ball and tossed it back to DeeJay.

"That's three out," DeeJay said.

Brody handed the bat to Rocco as DeeJay jogged in and handed the ball to Kal.

"You have to pitch to Rocco."

Kal felt a pang of nervousness. She hadn't pitched since she was in Halifax.

"What do you throw?" DeeJay asked.

"Fastballs," Kal said.

"That's it?"

"I have a palmball," Kal said.

"What's a palmball?" DeeJay said.

"I hold it like this." Kal showed DeeJay her grip on the ball using all five fingers.

"Oh, you mean a changeup."

"I call it a palmball."

"Does it work?"

"It's pretty dirty."

"Okay then. We'll start with fastballs. But if I drop two fingers, you fire me that dirty palmball."

Kal nodded.

"Let's switch gloves." DeeJay handed his glove to Kal.

Kal felt uncomfortable giving her glove to DeeJay. But she handed Trapper over.

Kal placed DeeJay's glove on her hand. It felt warm and a little clammy, but it fit.

Rocco stepped into the batter's box.

Kal wound up and delivered a fastball right down the middle.

*CRANK!* The ball shot off Rocco's bat and smashed into the wooden fence.

Kal didn't know how such a small kid could hit the ball so far.

"Homer! 2–0 for the good guys!" Brody yelled.

Then Kal threw the ball as hard as she could right down the middle.

*CRANK!* The ball flew off Rocco's bat and sailed over the wooden fence in left field.

"Another one! 3–0!" Brody shouted.

"This is too easy," Rocco shouted.

Kal began to worry. She'd thrown that pitch as hard as she could.

DeeJay ran up to Kal.

"You gotta hit the corners against these guys. Look where I place my glove and try to hit it," DeeJay said.

When DeeJay was back in position, he placed his glove on the outside corner of the plate.

Kal eyed his glove. She imagined she was throwing at a tree stump. Focused on hitting the glove, Kal wound up and delivered the pitch.

Rocco swung.

*Crank!* Rocco hit a pop fly to right field, and one of the boys in the field caught it easily.

"One out!" DeeJay shouted.

This time DeeJay placed his glove on the inside part of the plate.

Kal aimed at the glove and delivered the pitch.

Rocco swung and missed.

"That's two!" DeeJay shouted.

The boys in the field gasped. "C'mon, Rocco, you idiot. What are you swinging at that for?" Brody yelled.

DeeJay gave the signal for the palmball.

Kal gripped the ball tight in her hand. She wound up and delivered the pitch.

Rocco hesitated, and then swung hard. Just before the ball reached the plate, it dipped sharply. Rocco adjusted and was able to get his bat on it.

The ball rocketed directly at Kal. Without thinking, she held up her glove and caught the ball.

*Smack!* She hadn't even seen it enter her glove, but she could feel it in her palm.

"Whoa! Nice catch!" Kal heard the boys in the field shout.

"Sick pitch. That's three out. We're up," DeeJay said.

Brody took the mound.

"What was that last pitch you threw?" Rocco asked as Kal walked past.

"Palmball," Kal said.

"Dirty." Rocco grabbed his glove and crouched down behind the plate.

DeeJay handed Trapper back to Kal. "Nice glove," he said.

Kal smiled.

DeeJay picked up the bat and stepped into the batter's box. Brody wound up and delivered the pitch.

*CRANK!* The ball sailed high and deep to right field.

"Homer!" DeeJay yelled.

Brody slammed his hat on the ground. "I'm not even warm yet," he said.

Brody delivered another pitch. DeeJay swung hard.

*CRANK!* The ball sailed over the wooden fence in left field. The Trail Boys in the field cheered as one hopped the fence to retrieve the ball.

Kal was amazed at DeeJay's swing and his power. It looked like he was barely trying.

"3–2 game," DeeJay said.

Brody slammed his hat down on the ground again.

Rocco ran to the mound to talk with Brody. The two whispered, covering their mouths with their gloves to prevent anyone from reading their lips.

Rocco returned to the plate and crouched down.

Brody delivered the pitch. It was a curveball; Kal could tell by the spin on the ball.

DeeJay swung.

*Crank!* The ball shot straight up into the air and the first baseman caught it.

"One out!" Rocco shouted.

Brody wound up and delivered another curveball. DeeJay swung.

*Crank!* A ground ball to third base.

"Two out!" Rocco shouted.

Brody wound up and delivered a pitch, this time a fastball.

It seemed to catch DeeJay off guard, but he managed to hit it.

*Crank!* The ball lofted lazily into centre field and was caught.

"Three out!" Rocco shouted jumping to his feet.

DeeJay turned to Kal.

"Okay, Kal, you're up."

# 7 TOP OF THE FOURTH INNING: TATERTOWN

Brody handed the ball to Rocco and picked up his glove. "This should be good for some laughs, eh boys!" he said.

The boys in the field laughed some more. Rocco took the ball and headed to the mound.

Brody handed Kal an aluminium bat. But he held on tight until Kal made eye contact with him. Brody leaned in toward her, just inches away from her face. Kal thought he smelled like old tennis shoes.

"Try not to sissy up Hugo here," Brody snorted.

Kal looked around confused. "Who's Hugo?"

"That's my bat. His name is Hugo." Brody rolled his eyes as if Kal was just supposed to know.

Brody crouched down behind home plate and pounded his glove. "Come on, chick, we don't throw underhand and we don't have all day."

Kal took hold of Hugo the bat. She had always hated being called a chick. Why were girls chicks? Maybe guys had an animal nickname that used to be popular. How she'd love to call him some name, but she couldn't think of one. Another time.

Kal's clammy palms gripped the bat tight. It felt good in her fingers. She hadn't played baseball with anyone other than her dad and Joey since she had moved to Trail. A feeling of pure excitement swept over her as she gripped the bat in her hands and stepped into the batter's box. *Okay, Hugo, let's go.*

Kal turned to DeeJay. "Wait, where are the home runs?"

The boys in the field groaned.

"The wooden fence in left field and the tall brick wall in right are both tatertown. Got it?" Brody said impatiently.

"Tatertown?" Kal asked as she took a couple practice swings.

The boys in the field moaned.

"Tatertown is a home run. Geez!" Rocco yelled.

"Tatertown. Got it." Strange as it was, the lingo made sense to Kal. Home runs should have a special name to separate them from regular hits.

Kal pointed with Hugo to centre field at an old wooden shack. There were several rundown greenhouses in the yard, and beside the house was a tall dead pine tree. The yard was sealed off from the park with a tall chain fence.

"What about that house out there?" She asked.

Brody rolled his eyes and stood up.

"That's Ol' Man Shanklin's place. It's tatertown, too," DeeJay said.

"We've been breaking Ol' Shanklin's windows for years! That drunk old fart belongs in the loony bin," Brody said. He crouched back down behind the plate. "Oh, but don't worry, you can't hit it that far anyways. This isn't Valley Girl Practice!"

"I don't play for them," Kal said.

"Who do you play for?" Brody asked.

"No one," Kal said.

Kal stepped up to the plate. She went into the batting stance she'd learned from watching her favourite major league baseball player, Jose Bautista. She held her arms high, bent her knees and kept her weight on her back leg.

Rocco wound up and delivered the pitch right down the middle.

Kal tensed up. *Here it comes. Here it comes . . . Here it . . .* Kal stepped forward and swung and missed. The bat slipped out of her hands and flew all the way down to third base.

*Smack!* The ball hit Brody's glove and he tipped over backward in the dirt. He kicked his legs in the air, laughing heartily.

"Strike one! Are you having fun?"

The boys in the field laughed and began heckling Kal.

"This is too easy!" Rocco chirped to the boys in the field.

DeeJay retrieved the bat and jogged over, his long, blond hair bouncing beneath his baseball cap.

"Have another go, Kal. Chill though."

"Thanks."

Kal knelt down, picked up some dirt and rubbed it in her palms. She took a deep breath and her legs stopped shaking. The leftover cream cheese residue from her hair had stayed on her hands. It made the dirt stick to her palms, giving her extra grip. She twirled the bat in her hands and tapped the plate.

"Here comes strike two," Rocco joked. He wound up and delivered a pitch. Kal swung and missed.

"Two strikes!" Brody shouted.

Kal felt comfortable. She'd just missed making contact, and she'd be ready this time. Rocco wound up and delivered a pitch. Kal watched as the pitch came in right down the middle of the plate. She swung the bat, rolling her wrists and busting her hips.

*Crack!* The ball shot off her bat in a straight line to left field.

*Thump!* The ball took a couple of bounces in the grass before slamming up against the wooden fence. The boys in the field went dead silent.

"What's that?" Kal asked.

"Where did you say you were from?" Brody asked.

"Halifax."

"They suck over there," Brody said.

"That's an out," Rocco said.

"No one could have made a play on that laser. That's not an out!" DeeJay argued.

The Trail Boys in the field shouted in approval.

"Lucky hit," Brody grumbled.

Rocco glared at Kal and spat on the mound. "Lucky hit is right. This time, I ain't holding back."

Brody crouched down behind home plate. "Stop fooling around and hum ball, Rocco!"

*Hum ball.* Kal assumed Brody was telling Rocco to give her his best fastball.

Kal twirled the bat in her hands. She tapped it twice on home plate. Rocco wound up and fired a fastball. Kal didn't have time to think; she rocked forward and swung smoothly.

*CRANK!* This time she got all of it, hitting the ball with the fattest part of the bat.

DeeJay jumped up and down and pointed at Brody.

"Boom ohhh! She rocked him! That's a bomb!" DeeJay shouted.

"How about you shut the hell up, DeeJay!" Brody shouted back.

The ball soared high to centre field and deep into the blue sky before disappearing over Shanklin's fence.

*Smash!* The sound of glass breaking rang throughout the field.

"Tatertown!" Kal raised the bat in the air and shouted triumphantly.

Brody slammed his glove on the ground.

The field went silent for a moment, the boys all staring at the Shanklin place in shock.

A scruffy, grey-bearded old man appeared at the entrance. He had teeth that looked like baked beans and was limping toward the field.

Kal stared at the old man in disbelief. He was holding a pellet gun.

"Give me that!" Brody sneered as he angrily snatched Hugo out of Kal's sticky hands.

"Run! It's Shanklin!" The Trail Boys scattered instantly.

"This isn't over," Brody yelled at Kal as he raced off the field.

Kal hoped it wouldn't be. She might have made an enemy of Brody, but playing baseball with the Trail Boys had been the most fun she'd had since she'd been in Trail, or maybe ever.

*Bang! Bang!* Pellet gun blasts filled the air.

"You little punks! Quit breaking my windows!" Shanklin growled.

Kal covered her ears.

DeeJay grabbed Kal by the arm and smiled. "You should join our house league."

"Yeah?" Kal said.

"Yeah, but right now, you better get out of here." DeeJay took off running with the rest of the Trail Boys.

Kal snatched up her backpack and sprinted all the way home. She was scared and thrilled at the same time.

Kal burst through the doors of her house and ran through the living room. She ran straight into the kitchen. She stood in the kitchen, panting, trying to catch her breath. Kal's dad was dressed in his navy blue RCMP uniform.

He grabbed his lunchbox and put on his coat. "You're home late. Dinner is on the stove."

"Dad, wait." Kal still hadn't caught her breath.

"Whatever it is, it can wait till tomorrow. I have to head to work."

He looked Kal up and down. "What the — Is that cream cheese in your hair?" he asked.

Kal took a deep breath. "I want to play . . . I want to play baseball with the Trail Boys!"

# 8 BOTTOM OF THE FOURTH INNING: STRIKE ONE

*KNOCK! KNOCK!*

"Kal, are you up?"

*BUZZ!* Kal's phone rattled on her bedside table.

Kal rolled over in her bed. It was 10:30 a.m. on a PD day, which meant no school. Kal had hoped to sleep in until noon.

*KNOCK! KNOCK!*

"Kal!"

"What!" Kal shouted groggily.

"You have company!" her dad shouted from the other side of the door.

It was Tuesday. Sarah was picking her up to go to softball practice.

Kal thought about pretending to be sick. She didn't want to play softball with the Valley Girls.

"Kal! You have a friend waiting for you!" her dad shouted.

Kal jumped out of bed. One practice wouldn't hurt.

Moments later Kal rushed out the front door. It had

rained and everything was wet and soggy in the yard.

Kal waved goodbye to her dad as she ran by him where he was sitting on the porch, drinking coffee. She jumped into the red van parked in front of the house as he walked back inside.

"Finally!" Sarah said with a warm smile.

"Sorry I'm late. Slept in," Kal said.

"Hi there, KaLeah. Nice to meet you. Sarah has told me lots about you," Sarah's mom said from the driver's seat.

"Hi."

"Was that your father at the door?" Sarah's mother asked.

"Yes, ma'am," Kal said.

"Your dad is a cop?" Sarah asked.

"Yeah."

"Cool."

"I guess."

"So you moved here from Halifax?" Sarah's mother asked.

"Yes, ma'am."

"That's pretty far away."

"Yes, ma'am."

"Where's your mother?"

Kal paused for a moment. She didn't really know how to answer.

"Um. She's no longer with us, ma'am," Kal said.

"Oh. I'm sorry," Sarah's mom said.

Kal ignored Sarah's eyes on her and stared out the

window. There was a silence until they reached the ballpark. *At least the questions stopped*, thought Kal.

★★★

As soon as they got to the park, Sarah jumped out of the car and started running toward the field. "Hurry up, Kal, we're late."

Kal lagged behind. Up ahead, she could see Marcy, Jenny and Nikki dressed in full practice uniform, just like Sarah. They all wore green baseball pants, black-and-green jerseys and black mesh caps.

Kal felt out of place in her black sweatpants, a black long-sleeved dri-fit shirt and a white-and-blue baseball cap with the Blue Jays logo.

As Sarah approached the team, Marcy bowed to her.

"Ching chong, choo," Marcy said in a singsong fake Chinese accent.

The three girls snickered.

"Very funny," Sarah said.

"Hey, Kal, where are you in all of that black? Smile so we can see you," Nikki said.

The three girls laughed some more and walked away.

Kal refused to respond. The joke was so stupid. She'd heard it before and never understood it. She wasn't even that dark, not like her mother had been. She felt more and more like it was a mistake for her to be here.

*Tweet!*

A short woman with brown, bushy hair and glasses strutted onto the field, whistle hanging from her neck. Her jersey and shorts were so tight, Kal wondered how she'd managed to put them on.

"That's Miss Gibb. She's the coach," Sarah whispered to Kal.

"Obviously," Kal whispered back.

"Okay, ladies, we're going to take some ground balls, then some flies. Head out to the field," Miss Gibb shouted.

The Valley Girls and Kal took the field.

Miss Gibb hit ground balls and the girls practised their fielding.

When it came to Kal's turn, Miss Gibb stopped.

"Hi there!"

Kal waved.

"What's your name?"

"Kal."

"I'm Coach Gibb. Nice to meet ya. Here it comes, Kal."

*CRANK!* Miss Gibb hit a line drive to Kal's left.

"Oops, don't worry, I'll hit you another . . ."

Before Miss Gibb could finish her sentence, Kal had taken three strides to her left and dove into the air.

Kal snagged the ball out of mid-air. She landed on the ground and rolled to her knees. She fired a strike over to first base.

"Wow! Great play, Kal! I think we just found our shortstop!" Miss Gibb shouted.

"But that's Nikki's position," Kal heard Jenny say to Marcy.

Kal looked at Nikki. Nikki was glaring at her as she whispered to something to Marcy and Jenny. Kal decided to ignore her.

After the fielding was over, Miss Gibb split the girls up into teams.

Kal was happy to see that she and Sarah were on the same team. But she worried when Miss Gibb placed Nikki on the team, too. Jenny and Marcy were on the other team. Before Marcy ran out to first base, Nikki grabbed her and whispered something in her ear.

Marcy laughed and nodded. She smiled at Kal. It wasn't a friendly smile.

Kal was getting tired of all the whispering and laughing. She tried to ignore it and focus on playing.

"You're up, Sarah, then Kal, then Nikki. Jenny, you're pitching," Miss Gibb said.

Kal watched as Jenny went into a windmill wind-up and delivered the pitch to Sarah.

Sarah bunted the ball. She took off like a shot and beat out the throw to first base. Kal was surprised at what a fast runner Sarah was.

"Nice wheels, Sarah!" Kal shouted.

"Must be from doing all those Chinese food deliveries," Kal heard Nikki say to the players beside her.

A few of the girls laughed.

Kal shook her head. Nikki was going out of her way to be mean. And it seemed like no matter how stupid the joke, someone was going to laugh.

Kal stepped up to the plate.

She had to remember that it was softball, not baseball, like she was used to. The underhand pitch made the ball rise slightly.

Jenny wound up and delivered her first windmill pitch. Kal watched it go by.

"What's the matter, Kal — too fast for you?" Nikki said from the dugout.

Kal turned back to see that Nikki was filming her with her phone.

*I'll give her something to film,* Kal thought.

Jenny delivered her second windmill pitch.

Kal timed it perfectly and swung with everything she had.

CRANK! The ball jumped off Kal's bat and sailed deep to left field.

"Goodness gracious! You can sure hit!" Miss Gibb shouted.

But Kal was already running through the muddy infield. She watched the ball soar over the head of the left fielder and roll to the fence.

Kal rounded first base and was on her way to second. Suddenly, she felt Marcy's cleats against her shin. Before Kal knew what was happening, she was tumbling head over heels. She did a face plant into the mud.

Marcy had tripped her.

"Oops," Marcy said in a cute tone of voice.

"That dive was a perfect ten! Nice one, Kal," Nikki shouted.

Everyone in the field laughed at Kal. Even Sarah was giggling.

Kal looked at Nikki. She was smiling and she put her phone away.

Kal spat — some mud had gone into her mouth. Her entire front side was covered in mud.

"You and Marcy must have gotten tangled up there. Are you okay, Kal?" Miss Gibb asked.

Kal thought about grabbing Marcy by her ponytail and feeding her punches. But she wasn't worth it.

Dripping mud, Kal walked past first base and into the dugout.

"Kal?" Miss Gibb called after her. "Where you going, Kal?"

Kal grabbed her glove and her bag. She marched off the field.

"Kal!" Sarah called after her.

Kal ignored Sarah. Maybe Sarah was in on it. Maybe she brought her to the park to embarrass her to get in good with the Valley Girls.

Kal had had enough of softball and the Valley Girls for one day. She left the field and walked back to her house. Maybe she could get back to sleep.

# 9 TOP OF THE FIFTH INNING: DIGGING IN

Kal sat up in her bed, staring at her laptop in disbelief at Nikki's Instagram page. She'd been curious to find out who Nikki Collins really was. But now she regretted even opening her laptop. Over and over, her eyes scanned the page. As she read, more likes appeared on the screen.

Nikki Collins had posted a video.

The caption for the video read: "Watch Kal the clown. LMAO #loser."

Marcy had commented also saying: "How about that #clownnose LOL."

That nasty comment about her nose had likes.

Jenny commented: "When your clown shoes are too big. #Kaltheclown."

There were dozens of likes. It seemed everyone in her class had liked it.

The video played over and over again, showing Kal rounding first base and face planting into the mud.

No comment from Sarah Chong. Some friend she

had turned out to be. Kal was mad at herself for trusting Sarah. She should have known whose side Sarah would be on. After all, Kal was the new girl, and the Valley Girls were Sarah's teammates.

Kal's eyes filled with tears. Maybe she shouldn't have thrown the pudding on the bus. But would that have made any difference? The more Kal thought about it, the more the tears turned to anger. She began to wish she'd thrown something bigger and harder than pudding at the Valley Girls.

*Knock! Knock!*

"You awake, kiddo?" her dad called from behind the door.

Kal wiped the tears from her eyes. She slammed her laptop shut and slid it under her pillow before answering, "Yeah, come in."

Her dad walked into the room and sat down beside her. "How was softball practice today?"

She wanted to tell him about how mean the Valley Girls had been to her. She wanted to tell him about the bullying and Nikki's Instagram post. But she decided against it. The last thing she needed was for her dad to show up at the park like a super cop to fight her battles. That would only make things worse.

"Okay, I guess," Kal said.

"Good. I thought about what you said this afternoon, about playing baseball here. I heard they have a really good softball program; you don't want to try that instead?"

"No!" Kal snapped.

"Look, I see a lot of things on my patrol. It's this town, and some of these boys, well, they're a tough group. I want you to be really certain you want to do this because . . ."

"I don't need you to babysit me, Dad," Kal snapped. She felt the tears returning.

"What's your problem, sweetie?"

"I can take care of myself," Kal said angrily.

"Whoa, easy, Kal. I didn't say anything. I just asked if you're sure. Look, this isn't Halifax."

"I know that. I'm not stupid." Kal nodded.

"Hey! I don't like your tone or your attitude right now. You better correct yourself or we're going to have a problem."

Kal put her face in her pillow.

Her dad sighed and stood up. He walked over to the dresser and picked up a picture of Kal and her mother. "I wish you would talk to me, Kal. I know I'm not like Mom, but I'm trying here. You have to cut me some slack."

Kal slumped in her bed. She wished her mom was alive. She could talk to her mom about everything that was going on. Her mom would know what to do.

"Kal? Talk to me," her dad pleaded.

"I'm sorry, Dad. I'm just tired," Kal said through her pillow.

"Well, get some sleep. Tomorrow I'll take you to the

park and we'll get you registered on a house team for baseball."

"Thanks, Dad," Kal said quietly.

"Is everything all right, dear?" her dad asked.

Everything was far from all right. She dreaded going to school the next day. She was nervous about playing baseball with the boys. She missed Halifax and her old friends. Her whole world was upside down. Her dad couldn't possibly understand.

"I'm fine. I just miss Mom," Kal said.

"Me too, sweetie. Me too."

★★★

Kal's dad let her stay home from school the next day. Maybe he did understand a little. She slept in and watched TV until it was time to head to the ballpark for the start of the house baseball league.

He dropped her off and headed for work. Kal stretched in the field with the rest of the boys. They looked at her strangely. No one said a word to her.

When Brody and Rocco arrived, they laughed.

"Hey, clown!" Brody shouted.

A few of the boys chuckled.

Kal tried to ignore them and kept warming up.

When it came time to play catch with a partner, Kal looked around the field for someone who needed a partner. There was no one in sight. Some boys were even in groups of three. Kal was getting the message no one wanted to play with her.

"Hey, slugger!"

Kal whipped around. It was DeeJay.

"You got a partner?"

"You got a ball?" Kal said with a smile.

DeeJay flicked a baseball neatly out of his glove to Kal. If DeeJay had seen the video, he didn't seem to care about teasing her about it.

"Hey, thanks for letting me play the other day," Kal said.

"Yeah, I knew they didn't know you could hit. I wanted to shut Brody up."

Kal felt confused. Was DeeJay her friend? Or had he just used her to beat Brody?

Kal and DeeJay warmed up together. With each toss, he threw the ball at her harder. DeeJay had a powerful arm. Joey was the only person she'd seen throw the ball harder than DeeJay.

Kal returned the ball harder and faster, trying to keep pace with DeeJay.

"Okay, back up. Let's play some long toss," DeeJay said.

Kal backed up several metres.

"Too far for you?" Kal joked.

DeeJay laughed. He wound up and threw a strike across the field right to Kal.

Kal returned the ball to DeeJay with just as much zip.

"Nice arm," DeeJay yelled across the field.

*Tweet!* A man wearing a full baseball uniform with cleats appeared on the field. But his uniform hung loosely on his lean body. He looked like he was wearing pyjamas. Kal recognized the coach from the ghost infield. He put his fingers in his mouth and whistled again. He motioned everyone toward the dugout.

Kal and DeeJay jogged back into the field with the other boys.

"Who is that guy?" Kal said to DeeJay.

"That's Coach Smith. He's my dad," DeeJay said.

"Oh."

"It's the uniform, right? Dumb, I know. I get it from the guys all the time. Worst part is, he actually thinks it looks cool. It sucks having your dad as a coach of your house league team. And even worse is that he coaches the all-star team."

Kal was beginning to see why DeeJay had been left without a partner. The other boys made it hard for him because his dad was the coach.

"These are the teams for this year's Babe Ruth house league. Listen for your team," Coach Smith said. He adjusted his glasses and began reading the rosters of the teams.

"KaLeah Watson? Is this a misprint?" Coach Smith peered up from the list and scanned the group. When he finally fixed his gaze on Kal, he looked her up and down. He shook his head as he checked off her name.

When the uniforms were handed out, Kal was pleased to find she was on DeeJay's team. The uniform was black and red and had the name ATCO LUMBER across the front. But being on DeeJay's team meant that Coach Smith was going to be their coach.

# 10 BOTTOM OF THE FIFTH INNING: STRIKE TWO

"Let's play ball!" the umpire shouted.

The Atco Lumber team charged out onto the field, all except for Kal. Coach Smith had started her on the bench. Kal watched as DeeJay took the mound and warmed up.

Already she could see that Sam, the Atco Lumber catcher, could barely catch DeeJay's fastballs and was dropping every pitch. Kal knew she could do better as catcher.

"Hi, Kal!" a voice shouted. It was Sarah at the fence near the dugout.

Kal ignored her.

"Kal!" Sarah called.

Kal looked right at Sarah. Then she looked away as if she didn't know her.

Sarah looked hurt and walked away.

Kal looked up to see her dad in the stands staring right at her. He gave a look that said "don't worry." And he mouthed the words "be ready."

Kal nodded and began cheering on her teammates. Atco Lumber was facing Big O Tire, the team Brody and Rocco played for.

Kal watched from the bench as the first two innings went by. Coach Smith barely said a word to her. In fact, no one on the team said anything to her, except DeeJay, who high-fived her every time he came into the dugout.

At the start of the third inning, with the score tied 2–2, DeeJay struck out the first batter on fastballs.

"That's the way, DeeJay!" Kal shouted.

The next batter up was Rocco. DeeJay started to lose control of his pitches. He threw four straight balls and walked Rocco.

"Settle down, son!" Coach Smith shouted.

DeeJay continued to struggle. He walked the second batter, putting runners on first and second base. DeeJay's next pitch got past Sam the catcher. That allowed the runners on first and second to advance.

"Come on, Sam, you've got to squeeze that baseball!" Coach Smith shouted at the catcher.

"Go ahead and yell at him, Smitty, he knows better. You know better, don't you, son!" A man with a large belly and large beard shouted to Sam from the side of the dugout.

DeeJay's next pitch went off Sam's glove all the way to the backstop. Rocco sped home and scored on the play. The score was 3–2 for Big O Tire.

"That kid can't catch a cold," Rocco shouted happily to his teammates as he ran back to the dugout.

On the next pitch, the Big O Tire batter bunted the ball and it rolled just in front of the plate.

Sam flicked off his mask and charged after the ball. He scooped it up and threw it way over the first baseman's head into right field.

Coach Smith angrily slammed his hat down on the dugout floor. Another run crossed the plate, making it 4–2 for Big O Tire.

Finally, DeeJay struck out Brody with a nasty curveball.

"Nice one!" Kal shouted.

Brody slammed his bat in the dirt and threw his helmet in disgust.

DeeJay walked straight to his dad in the dugout. He whispered something in Coach Smith's ear.

"You just worry about your pitching; I'll do the coaching! Your pitching is terrible right now!" Coach Smith snapped back. DeeJay tried to walk away, but Coach Smith grabbed him by the arm and shouted at him some more.

Kal had been using her time on the bench. She watched closely how the players played, how they pitched and how they moved. Just in case she got her chance to play, she wanted to be ready. The way Coach Smith was, she knew she'd better be focused. There were some good players back in Halifax, but Trail had great players.

Rocco was one of them.

Rocco was pitching for Big O Tire. He strutted about the mound and made jokes with his teammates in the field.

As soon as the first batter stepped into the batter's box, Rocco started firing strikes. He struck out three Atco Lumber batters in a row with just nine pitches. None of them even made contact with the ball.

Before Kal's team could charge back onto the field for the fourth inning, Coach Smith called everyone together.

"Okay, we're making some changes. Brian, you're in for Ian. Sam, you're out. KaLeah, you're in at catcher. Get suited up." He didn't look happy to tell her that.

Kal's hands trembled as she strapped on the shin pads. DeeJay handed her a catcher's mask and tapped his glove on her chest protector.

"You taking my son out for her? You're making a big mistake, Smitty," Sam's father barked at Coach Smith.

"I don't want to hear it, Davis," Coach Smith shouted back.

Kal flipped her cap backward and slipped the catcher's mask over her face. A rush of excitement swept over her. This was her chance.

Her arm felt good. She felt good. The sun was shining. After catching some warm-up pitches from DeeJay, sweat was pouring down her brow and her heart was racing. She was finally in the game.

DeeJay seemed to be pumped up, too. He struck out the first batter on three straight pitches.

The second batter swung on the first pitch.

*Crank!* The ball looped behind the plate and soared toward the backstop.

Kal started tracking the ball as soon as it was hit. She ripped off her catcher's mask and sprinted toward the stands. Just before she reached the backstop, Kal slid on her knees and caught the ball.

"Out!" the umpire shouted.

"Nice play, Kal!" her teammates shouted.

Kal flashed a smile and held two fingers in the air, signalling two out.

DeeJay struck out the next batter.

As the game progressed, Kal hit two singles off Rocco. She drove in a run and stole a base.

In the field she was solid. Kal blocked pitches in the dirt with her body and threw out two runners attempting to steal bases on her. Every time she came into the dugout, the other boys on her team tapped their gloves against her shin pads or her chest protector.

At the bottom of the seventh inning, Atco Lumber's last at bat, the game was tied 4–4.

Rocco gave up a base hit to the first Atco Lumber batter and walked the next two to load the bases. It was Kal's turn to bat.

As she walked toward the batter's box, the Big O

Tire coach called timeout to make a pitching change.

Brody jogged in and took the mound. He sized Kal up in between pitches as he warmed up.

Nervousness swept through Kal. She knew Brody could throw really hard, almost as hard as DeeJay.

DeeJay stood on deck behind Kal. "Here we go, Kal, wait for your pitch!" he cheered.

Kal picked up some dirt and rubbed it in her hands. She took a few practice swings and then stepped into the batter's box.

"Play ball," the umpire shouted.

Brody fired the first pitch right down the middle.

Kal just watched as the ball thudded against the catcher's glove.

"Strike one!" the umpire hollered.

Brody fired another pitch.

*Thud!*

"Steeeeeerike two," the umpire shouted.

Kal had watched the first two pitches zoom past her. But now she had the timing down.

Brody wound up and threw another pitch. This time, Kal swung.

*Crack!* The ball sailed high and deep down the left field line. Kal took off running, sure she'd hit her first Babe Ruth league home run.

Kal watched as the ball hooked just past the foul pole and over the left field fence.

"Foul ball!" the umpire shouted.

Kal had just missed hitting a grand-slam home run to win the game. As she made her way back to the plate, she saw that Marcy, Jenny and Nikki had joined Sarah in the stands.

"Strike her out, Brody!" Nikki, Jenny and Marcy shouted from the stands.

Rocco ran to the mound from shortstop. "C'mon, Brody, do this!" Rocco pleaded.

"I got it," Brody said, giving Kal an angry look.

Kal picked up her bat. She couldn't think about the missed home run or the Valley Girls. All she needed was a single to win the game for her team.

"Let's go, Kal," she heard her dad shout.

Brody fired another pitch. The ball was speeding directly at Kal. Kal turned her head away and braced for the impact.

DOOP! The ball hit Kal square between her shoulder blades.

Kal fell to one knee. Shock waves of pain shot through her entire body from where the ball had hit her. Her hands went numb and she began to tremble.

Tears welling in her eyes, Kal dropped to the ground and writhed in pain.

A hush went over the crowd.

Kal gasped for air. She was sobbing so hard she was having trouble breathing.

"Stand back — everyone clear away!" Kal heard a voice say.

Kal looked up to see her dad kneeling over her. She wanted to get up, but she felt paralyzed by the pain. Tears streamed down her face.

She could hear Sam's dad shouting, "This is exactly what can happen when a girl plays out here with these boys. You did this, Smitty!"

Murmurs spread across the crowd.

"She shouldn't be playing," Kal heard a woman's voice say.

"It's a dangerous game," Kal heard a man say.

Kal's dad picked her up in his arms and carried her off the field.

# 11 TOP OF THE SIXTH INNING: DOWN BUT NOT OUT

Kal rolled over in her bed. Her back ached. She flipped through the channels looking for an interesting reality TV show. She loved reality TV. Unable to find anything, Kal turned to a music channel but frowned. The channel was playing some sitcom, not music videos. She could have really used a good song to lift her spirits. She sat up and removed the bag of ice her dad had strapped to her back with plastic wrap. She tossed it to the floor.

Kal didn't know how she could face the Trail Boys or the Valley Girls. She'd been humiliated by the Valley Girls and she'd cried in front of the Trail Boys. It just made things worse that her dad had had to carry her off the field.

Sadness and anger swept over Kal. *Brody meant to hit me,* Kal thought. *Now they all think I don't belong on the team.*

Kal opened her laptop. She opened Nikki's Instagram page, and her worst fears came to life right before her eyes. Nikki had posted a video of the moment Kal was hit by a pitch. Nikki had created a Vine, a constant loop showing Kal being hit with the pitch and lying in the dirt, crying. It repeated over and over again. The caption beside the post read: "Another clown act LOL #loser." No doubt she had also posted it on her Snapchat account and sent it to everyone.

Kal didn't bother to read the rest of the comments. It was probably just people making fun of her. She was glad her dad let her skip school again. If she could, she'd never go back there.

Kal wiped tears from her eyes.

*Knock! Knock!*

"Kal, are you up?" her dad called from behind the door.

"Don't come in — I'm changing," Kal lied.

"There's a boy outside," he said through the door. "I can tell him to leave if you're not feeling well."

"Who is it?"

"He said his name is Joey. Want me to tell him to beat it?"

"No, Dad. I'll be down in a minute." Kal ran to her bathroom mirror. Her eyes were bloodshot from crying. Kal splashed some water on her face, tied her hair in a ponytail and applied some lip gloss.

"You sure? I could cuff him for you and you could bust his nose."

"Dad!"

"I'm just saying."

Kal finished getting herself ready, grabbed her glove and ran outside to meet Joey.

"Hey, you look like crap!" Joey exclaimed.

"Thanks, Joey."

"Jokes. You want to play catch or something?"

"Sure."

The two headed to a ballpark Kal had never been to. The dugouts were old and rundown. The grass had grown over the infield but the pitching mound and plate were still visible.

"What is this place?" Kal asked.

"This used to be where everyone played, until they built the new park. No one comes here anymore. Except me."

Kal knelt down behind the plate. The backstop was covered in graffiti. And the dirt was hard like clay.

Joey pitched to Kal. He worked on his curveball and Kal practised blocking and catching his pitches.

"You know, you were really good back there," Joey said, wiping the sweat from his brow.

"Thanks."

"No, seriously," Joey said.

"Really?" Kal was shocked. Joey was maybe the best kid player she'd ever seen, and he thought she was good.

"Yeah." Joey looked down at his shoes and walked toward her.

Kal stood up, removed her hat and wiped the sweat

from her brow with her T-shirt. Her heart began to race. Joey had a look on his face that Kal didn't recognize.

Joey was breathing heavily. He reached out and ran his fingers through Kal's hair.

"Your hair is so cool."

Kal untied her hair and let it fall down just above her shoulders.

"I hate it."

"Why? It's pretty."

Joey smiled and looked into Kal's eyes.

Kal's legs felt wobbly. Was Joey going to kiss her? Had this been why he'd brought her to this park? She didn't know what to do. Should she close her eyes?

Kal smiled back nervously.

Joey seemed to lose his nerve. "Hey, you want to see something cool?" he asked.

Relief swept over Kal. "Sure." *What could it be?* she wondered.

"Follow me. We'll have to hurry, though," Joey said.

Joey jogged off the field. Kal ran after him.

They ran several blocks. Kal did her best to keep up with Joey.

As they ran through the Trail streets, cars drove by and honked. Kal began to feel awkward. Why was every car honking at them?

"What's going on?" Kal asked.

"What?"

"Why are people honking at us?"

"They're honking at me."

A truck rolled by and the driver rolled down his window and shouted, "Joey, we're all pulling for you guys this year!"

Joey waved back.

Kal felt like she was with a celebrity. Why did everyone know Joey?

They ran up to a large building. In front of the building was the statue of a gladiator holding a trophy. HOME OF CHAMPIONS was written on the base of the statue. The building had a sign over the door that read TRAIL MEMORIAL CENTRE.

"C'mon, they'll be closing soon," Joey said as Kal followed him inside.

They hurried into a foyer. Below the foyer was a large ice hockey rink with several banners of titles the team had won. TRAIL SMOKE EATERS was written on the ice in the centre of the rink.

"This way," Joey said.

Joey led Kal up some stairs. At the top of the stairs, the room opened into a large hallway. On each wall were large glass cases filled with hundreds of golden trophies and plaques and black-and-white photos.

"What is this place?" Kal said.

"This is the Trail Hall of Fame," Joey said.

Kal looked around at the trophies and plaques.

"They used to call this town the Home of Champions," Joey said. "My coach says our team has what it takes, if I just pitch like I can. That we can be champions."

Kal could tell that doing well in sports was all Joey thought about.

"Take a look at this." Joey called her over to a large glass case. In it was a black-and-white photo of a hockey team. WORLD CHAMPIONS was written on the plaque.

"They were a bunch of local boys who won the world hockey championships a long time ago. They beat the Russians when no one else in the world could," Joey said.

"Cool," Kal said. She didn't know much about hockey, but it sounded pretty amazing that some guys from Trail were world champions.

"Come check this out. This is what I wanted to show you," Joey said.

Kal followed Joey to another display case. She looked through the glass at a newspaper clipping. It was a picture of a tall girl with long, blond hair. She was pitching. She had Trail All-Stars written across her chest.

"Who is she?" Kal asked.

"That's Kelly Craig. She's also in the Canadian Baseball Hall of Fame."

"Really?"

"Yes, her team played in the Little League World Series."

# Top of the Sixth Inning: Down but Not Out

Kal looked over the old picture again. Her mind raced.

"That was almost thirty years ago. But when I saw the *Trail Times* today, I thought you should see this."

"What was in the *Trail Times*?" Kal asked.

"You didn't see the paper today?!"

"No. Why?"

Joey grabbed Kal by the arm and led her down the stairs. He grabbed a newspaper from the recycling bin and flipped through it.

"Check this out!" Joey handed the paper to Kal.

Kal looked in awe at the picture on the page. It showed her being hit by the pitch. The title read: "STANDOUT TAKES ONE FOR TEAM."

The article went on to describe how well Kal had played. It compared her to Kelly Craig, the Hall of Famer. A smile swept across Kal's face as she read the article. She hadn't even asked what happened in the game. When she was hit by the pitch, she had been credited with driving in a run. It won the game for her team. *She* won the game for her team.

"Got some good ink in there, Kal," Joey said.

"Thanks, Joey," Kal said.

# 12 BOTTOM OF THE SIXTH INNING: HANGING WITH THE TRAIL BOYS

Kal and Joey jogged to the park. The sun was so hot, it was hard to breathe. When they reached the park, they found DeeJay, Rocco, Brody and the rest of the Trail Boys sitting in the shade.

"Who invited her?" Brody muttered under his breath.

"Shut your mouth, Brody, before I punch it," Joey said.

Brody put his head down.

"What's up, Joe?" DeeJay said.

"Hey, my man. You guys going to play or what?"

"I don't know if we have it in us. These boys are being sissies because of the heat."

"That's weak. Where's all the older cats? I was supposed to catch up with my bros here," Joey said.

"Oh, yeah, they were here. They left and went to some birthday party," Brody said.

"Did I say you could talk, fat boy?" Joey snapped at Brody.

Brody put his head back down.

"Yeah, they just left a few minutes ago. I think they were heading up to Fort Shepherd, some huge bush party," DeeJay said.

"Oh shit. I'm supposed to be there."

"Are you leaving, Joey?" Kal asked.

"Yeah, I have to take the wood pallets for the fire. I'll catch up with you later, Kal," Joey said casually.

The nervous and sensitive Joey Kal had been with all morning was gone.

Kal nodded. "Cool."

"Brody, you got anything for me?" Joey said.

Brody removed a can of chewing tobacco from his pocket and tossed it to Joey. "It's a full can," he said. "I grabbed it from my old man's stash."

"I'm keeping this," Joey said.

"Hey, no problem, Joey. I can get you another one tomorrow if you want," Brody said.

"Later, Joey," DeeJay said, patting Joey on the back.

"Later, Joey," Rocco and Brody chimed in, smiling from ear to ear.

Joey gave the Trail Boys a nod and jogged off.

"He's so cool, man," Rocco said to Brody.

"I know, that's why I gave him my tin. He'll re-member that," Brody said.

"He doesn't even like you guys," DeeJay said.

"Yeah, he does. He took my tin," Brody said.

Kal was a little thrown by the way the Trail Boys

treated Joey. It was as if he was a hero to them. She remembered how everyone in town seemed to know him. But with Joey gone, she also felt a little uncomfortable. How would the Trail Boys be with her after her being hit by the pitch?

"What's up, Kal? You all right?" DeeJay said, standing up.

Kal could relax around DeeJay. He looked at her like she was one of the boys. He treated her like a friend.

"I'm cool," Kal said.

"It's too hot," Rocco said, wiping sweat from his brow.

"Let's go down to the river!" Brody shouted.

"I'm in," Rocco said.

The rest of the Trail Boys followed them out of the park.

"You coming, Kal?" DeeJay asked.

"Sure, I guess," Kal said. She was happy they weren't making fun of her, especially Brody. She'd expected them to jump all over her as soon as Joey left. But it was almost like the derby and the game hadn't happened.

Kal followed as the boys walked down a steep dirt path. The path opened into a clearing beside a very swift moving river.

The boys took their shirts off and tied them around their arms.

Kal kept staring at the rushing water. There were swirling whirlpools and large rocks jutting out from it.

What were they doing here?

"What'sa matter, Kal? Scared?" Brody said with a sneer.

"Yeah, Kal, you scared?" laughed Rocco.

*Here we go*, Kal thought. *He's going to start in on how he hit me with the pitch and I cried.*

"She wasn't too scared to wear one of your fastballs, Brody. And, Rocco, you would have ducked out of the way and squealed like a little pig. That's what you did when I threw at you last year!" DeeJay answered.

"That's because I bruise easily, DeeJay. And I have asthma," Rocco replied.

All the boys groaned in protest at Rocco's lame defence.

"There he goes with his asthma again," DeeJay snorted.

"I'll show you my puffer!" Rocco pleaded.

"All right, I'll give you some props, Kal," Brody said. "But we're still going to beat Atco Lumber in the playoffs," Brody said.

"Whatever, Brody!" DeeJay shouted.

Kal was amazed at the way the boys quickly backed down when challenged by Joey and DeeJay — her friends. Kal saw that her friends didn't lose respect for her when she was hit by the pitch. They saw it as an act of bravery.

"You coming in?" DeeJay asked. He pointed to the swirling whirlpools. "Those are the Onions. It's like a water slide. Once you jump in, just make sure you swim hard enough to fight the current. If you can get to the Onions, they'll just pull and spin ya back to the beach. It's super fun."

"You have to swim hard early or the current will pull you out to the middle of the river," Rocco added. "And that will be it for you. I heard the last person who got swept away was found all chopped up by the US border down the river."

"Probably got chewed up by the dam down there or the monster sturgeon fishes," Brody said.

"You guys are full of it," DeeJay said. "Don't mind them, Kal. They never actually found the body."

"That's reassuring," Kal said.

"Just keep your knees up or those rocks will get ya," Brody added.

"Yeah, that's how I got this scar." Rocco showed Kal a long scar on his knee.

"I'll see you losers at the beach," Brody shouted and jumped into the raging river.

One by one the Trail Boys jumped in to the river while still wearing their shoes and baseball caps.

"Come on, Kal, it's fun," DeeJay said.

Kal stood there weighing her options. If she didn't jump in, they would think she was a coward. And all the respect they had for her bravery on the field could be lost. If she did jump in, she could end up drowned and floating by the US border or eaten by monster sturgeon fish.

Kal jumped in.

She felt a rush as she jumped into the water. The water was cold, but very refreshing.

"Swim!" DeeJay shouted back at her.

Kal realized she was being pulled off course toward the middle of the river.

"Swim harder," DeeJay yelled.

Kal began swimming as hard as she could, waving her hands frantically. She could feel the strength of the current pulling her. She began kicking her legs and paddling with her hands as hard as she could. Slowly, she began to make her way toward the Onions.

Suddenly, Kal felt her body being pulled toward the swirling whirlpools. Kal watched as DeeJay went through the first whirlpool. It sucked him under the water and he disappeared. Kal watched in shock, waiting for him to reappear. He didn't. Kal was horrified. *No wonder they called it the Onions*: Kal felt like crying.

Before she realized, Kal was being spun around by a whirlpool. She pulled her knees up and dodged a large rock. The next whirlpool pulled her under. Water rushed up her nose and Kal began to choke. Suddenly, she was above the water again, spinning, and being whisked toward the beach.

Kal arrived at the beach and crawled out of the water.

COUGH! River water spewed out of Kal's nose and mouth.

She looked around for DeeJay. *Maybe he'd been swept out?*

"Fun, wasn't it?" a voice said from down the riverbank.

DeeJay ran over to Kal.

"I thought you went under," Kal said, still trying to catch her breath.

"Yeah, one of those whirlpools got me!" DeeJay said excitedly.

Kal rose to her feet. She couldn't believe what she had just done. Her heart was pounding in her chest from excitement and fear. She was not as strong a swimmer as the rest of the boys, so for her, it had been more terrifying than fun.

★★★

Kal walked with the Trail Boys through the city streets. The sun completely dried her clothes in just minutes. The only evidence that she had been swimming in raging rapids was the squishy sound her shoes were making.

DeeJay checked his wristwatch. "Oh man. I gotta go, my mom is going to kill me. See ya'll later." He sprinted off.

"What's up with him?" Kal asked Rocco.

"He's got piano lessons," Rocco said.

"Piano lessons? What a loser. That guy thinks he's

freakin' Beethoven or some crap," Brody said.

Kal thought it was cool that DeeJay could play the piano. But she decided not to challenge Brody without DeeJay around.

"Hey, guys, let's go up to Shaver's Bench and bomb cars!" Brody said.

The rest of the Trail Boys excitedly agreed.

Kal wasn't sure what Brody was talking about, but it didn't sound like a good idea. A little curious, and still wanting to fit in, Kal followed along. Maybe if she showed Brody she could hang out with them, he'd stop trying to put her down all the time.

"Let's hit up Chong's first!" Brody said.

"Yeah!" the rest of the Trail Boys shouted.

Kal had no idea what Brody meant this time either, but she followed along.

# 13 TOP OF THE SEVENTH INNING: BAD COMPANY

Kal followed the Trail Boys to a small convenience store. They all piled into it.

Kal didn't have any money, so she decided to just stand by the door.

A lean Chinese man stood up from a chair behind the counter. "Can I help you, young lady?" he asked.

Kal spotted one of the Trail Boys stuffing a chocolate bar into his shorts.

"Young lady?" the man asked.

"Oh, sorry, I'm just looking," Kal said.

Out of the corner of her eye, Kal could see Brody, Rocco and the rest of the Trail Boys filling their pockets with candy. Kal couldn't believe it. They were stealing.

Kal looked at the man behind the counter. She realized he would have to look around the magazine racks to see the Trail Boys. And he was focused on her.

"I haven't seen you in here before. Are you new to this town?" he asked.

Kal tried not to stare at Brody. He was grabbing

anything he could get his hands on.

Kal felt scared, nervous and embarrassed all at once.

"Uh, yeah, I just moved here. From Halifax."

"Oh, what grade are you in?"

"Eighth grade, sir."

"Oh, you must know my daughter, Sarah."

Kal looked at the pictures hanging on the wall behind the counter. In among the smiling images was a familiar face. It was Sarah. Kal felt sick to her stomach. The man was Sarah's dad. Chong's was Sarah's dad's store.

"Um, ya."

"C'mon, let's go!" Brody shouted.

The rest of the Trail Boys ran out of the store, leaving Kal behind.

Kal expected Mr. Chong to run after the boys or call the police. She froze.

"Those boys are bad news," Mr. Chong said, shaking his head.

Kal shrugged her shoulders and pretended she didn't know what he was talking about.

"Are you sure you don't want anything, young lady?"

"No, thank you, sir. I forgot my money at home."

"You can grab a pop on the house, since you're new to this town. It's hot outside, you know," Mr. Chong said with a smile.

Mr. Chong grabbed a pop from the fridge and

handed it to Kal. "Here you go."

"Thanks." Kal felt terrible.

"You're tall, young lady. You should play softball with my daughter, Sarah. They have a really good softball team in this town. We win a lot of championships," Mr. Chong said.

"Oh, okay. Well, thanks for the pop, sir."

"You're welcome."

Kal hustled out of the store.

As soon as she got outside, she looked around, but there was no sight of the Trail Boys.

Kal began walking home. She walked a few blocks sipping her pop and thinking about what had just happened. Mr. Chong hadn't realized she was with the Trail Boys. She'd been lucky.

"Hey, Kal!" Rocco shouted.

Kal turned her head. The Trail Boys were sitting in an alley eating candy.

"You guys left me!" Kal said.

They jumped up and surrounded her.

"We thought you were right behind us," Rocco said.

"Well, I wasn't," Kal said. She was about to say more, but Brody took a step toward her.

"Hey, Kal, that was really freaking cool what you did, distracting Chong while we boosted the store. You've got more balls than DeeJay, that's for sure. Want some candy?" Brody said.

Brody held out a sweaty palm filled with jawbreakers.

Kal shook her head. There was no way she was eating anything that came out of that palm.

"You're a pro, Kal. That was the easiest boost we've ever done," Brody said.

"Yeah, Kal!" the rest of the Trail Boys chimed in.

"Yeah, well." Kal hated taking credit for something she was ashamed to be a part of. But maybe she could use the fact that the Trail Boys were happy with her to understand what was going on.

"Rocco, can I ask you something?" Kal whispered as they walked along.

"Shoot," Rocco said.

"Why don't you guys like DeeJay?" Kal asked.

Rocco looked confused. "Whaddya mean?"

"I don't know. I just thought . . ." Kal said.

"No, we're all friends. DeeJay and Brody have been going at it since kindergarten. But they both really want to be best. We beat Atco Lumber at Silver City Days last year, and Brody got MVP. DeeJay was pretty pissed."

Kal nodded.

"I could have easily been the MVP, too," said Rocco. "I was killing in that tourney. But politics, Kal. Politics," Rocco said.

"Politics?"

"Yup. A lot of politics," Rocco said.

Kal nodded. She knew all too well.

"What's that, Rocco?" Brody said.

"Nothing, Brody. Hey, Kal, did you see that you were in the paper?" Rocco asked.

Before Kal could respond, Brody interrupted. "Oh please! Like there's something special about being in a piece of crap like the *Trail Times*. I should be in the paper every week."

"Yeah, I saw it, Rocco," Kal said, ignoring Brody's outburst.

Rocco gave her a quick smile through his braces.

Kal smiled back at Rocco. He didn't dislike her as much as Brody did! But he seemed to follow whatever Brody said and did.

Brody led the Trail Boys and Kal up a winding road that wrapped around a small hill. At the top of the road was a quiet neighbourhood filled with fruit trees.

The Trail Boys ran to the trees and started filling their pockets with unripe plums, crabapples and pears.

Rocco handed Kal a plum. It was green and as hard as a rock.

"This way!" Brody led them toward a bank that looked out over the highway.

A red car drove past below them. The boys threw fruit from the hill top toward the car. A few crab apples and a pear hit the car as it sped past.

SPLAT!

HONK! The car horn wailed.

"Nailed him. Here comes another one," Brody said.

A black truck with huge tires roared past below.

"Now!" Brody instructed.

Kal looked down at the plum in her hand.

The boys threw again.

KA-SPLAT! This time several pieces of fruit pinged off the side and top of the truck.

SCREECH! The truck swerved and the driver slammed on the brakes. The truck came to a halt. The boys ducked down below the bushes.

Kal ducked down, too. But she could hear the driver screaming from the road below.

Brody peeked his head up and tossed more fruit. Kal heard a car door shut and the roar of an engine as the truck sped away.

Brody and the rest of the Trail Boys thought the whole thing was hilarious. Kal didn't see anything funny or fun about what they were doing. This was the kind of thing her dad arrested people for. So was what they had done at Chong's.

A minivan rolled slowly past. From the distance, Kal could see a woman driving. Two little kids sat in kiddy seats in the back seat.

Kal felt the rock-hard green plum in her hand. She thought about how the truck had swerved and almost driven off the road.

"Easy target, boys," Brody said.

Kal stood up and began walking away.

"Where you going?" Rocco asked.

Kal didn't say a word. She just kept walking. How

could she be a part of this?

"Let her go. She doesn't have the balls to hang out anyways," Brody said.

"Screw you, Brody!" Kal shouted back. She wheeled around and fired the plum in Brody's direction.

The plum whizzed past Brody's head and slammed into a tree just above his head.

"Hey! Get back here!" Brody shouted.

Kal took off running.

# 14 BOTTOM OF THE SEVENTH INNING: EASY OUT

Kal ran past the empty softball field as she sprinted home. Out of the corner of her eye, she saw a dark-haired girl in a baseball uniform. She was sitting by herself in the dugout. Kal slowed down. It was Sarah. Where were her Valley Girl friends?

As Kal neared the dugout, she could hear Sarah sobbing as she talked on the phone. Kal waited for her to end the conversation.

"Can't you just come pick me up now, Mom? I don't know, just come get me, please. Okay, I'll wait here." Sarah hung up her phone and looked up to see Kal.

"Hey," Sarah said sadly, unable to control her sobs.

"Hey," Kal answered. "Where is everyone?" Kal asked as she sat down beside Sarah.

"Marcy, Jenny and Nikki lied to me. They told me we had a make-up game today that wasn't on the schedule. I'm so stupid. They're probably all having a really good laugh right now."

Kal shook her head. "What are you going to do?"

"I'll just wait here until my mom can leave work to pick me up. I don't want anyone else to see me crying. My Mom's not happy, either. Can you believe she's actually blaming me for what they did?" Sarah said, getting even more upset.

"Well, let's play catch or something while you wait," Kal said.

"Really?" Sarah said.

"Why not?" Kal felt sorry for Sarah. What the Valley Girls had done was a mean prank. Kal also felt bad that she had helped the Trail Boys rob Sarah's dad's store, even though she never meant to.

Sarah grabbed her glove and a softball. The two girls walked out on the field and began playing catch.

They played in silence for a few moments. "Why do you put up with them?" Kal asked.

"Put up with who?" Sarah asked.

"Nikki, Jenny and Marcy."

"I don't know. They're my friends," Sarah said.

"They don't act like they're your friends," Kal said.

"They've always been like that," Sarah said.

"Why don't you ever say anything?" Kal asked. "Like, stick up for yourself."

"That's easy for you to say. Everyone sticks up for you," Sarah said.

"What are you talking about? What do you mean, everyone sticks up for me?"

"I saw it on Instagram. I'll show you." Sarah ran to the dugout and retrieved her phone.

She opened up Nikki's Instagram page and showed Kal. "I don't want to see this," Kal said. She had already seen the Vine. How could Sarah call that sticking up for her?

"Follow the comments," Sarah insisted.

The first few comments were Marcy and Jenny, poking fun. But then there was a comment from someone named Joe Smoke. It read, "Nikki you're the loser."

"See, if you click on Joe Smoke, here's his Instagram page."

On the page was the picture of Kal on the front page of the newspaper. Joe Smoke's page had thousands of followers — probably everyone in the town.

Kal began reading the comments that followed the Joe Smoke post. Several of the Trail Boys had jumped in and blasted @prittynikki11 for posting the Vine. DeeJay was one of them.

DeeJay had written, "Kal won the game for us. You're just a #hater!"

There were negative comments saying Nikki was jealous. There were insults directed at Nikki for posting the Vine. So many, Kal couldn't read them all. Sarah scrolled down to the last comment.

@prittynikki11 had written back to @JoeSmoke. "I was just joking. Kal is one of my friends."

Kal was shocked. How could Nikki say they were

friends? They were enemies.

"How do you know Smoke?" Sarah asked.

"Who is Smoke?"

"I think that's just his nickname. His real name is Joey Neufeld. He's like the greatest hockey and baseball player in the province. He's probably going to the NHL or the Major Leagues, whichever he wants. I can't believe he stuck up for you. Here's a picture of him pitching. Do you know him?" Sarah asked.

"Oh! Joey? He lives down the street from me," Kal said.

"Well, he's only the most popular guy in Trail. He's a ninth grader but even the twelfth graders respect him. All the girls in our school have the biggest crushes on him. Especially Nikki. She's got newspaper clippings of him plastered all over the walls in her room," Sarah said.

"Really? Joey?" Kal said, laughing.

"Yeah. He posted on Nikki's page to defend you."

"Wow," Kal said.

"All the girls were talking about it at school. Everyone saw you in the paper and heard about what Joe wrote on Nikki's page. You're, like, super popular at school now," Sarah said.

"Really?" Kal was stunned. How could she have gone from a nobody new kid to a popular girl just because of Joey?

"Yeah. You're lucky. This is what Nikki posts about me." Sarah showed Kal her phone.

Kal looked at the posts Nikki, Jenny and Marcy had made about Sarah on Instagram. They were all very mean. Some made fun of her being Chinese.

"Texts, too." Sarah showed Kal group chats where Marcy, Jenny and Nikki just poked fun at Sarah for anything and everything. There was even a really mean meme that showed Sarah's face on the body of a donkey.

"You won't believe the prank videos they post of me on Snapchat."

"Geez," Kal said. Kal had thought she had it bad, but Sarah had it worse. And Sarah still thought she was supposed to be their friend.

"Ever since they became seniors at middle school, it's gotten worse. They run the whole school and they do that to everyone, basically. It's mostly Nikki, with Marcy and Jenny just following along. When Nikki's not around, they don't bug me at all. I guess they're just playing around," Sarah said.

"I thought you were just like them," Kal admitted.

"Is that why you started ignoring me?" Sarah asked.

Kal felt bad for grouping Sarah together with the Valley Girls. Kal realized that for the Valley Girls, Sarah was an easy target to pick on, *an easy out*.

Kal remembered how lonely and sad she had felt when she didn't have any friends at all. But was it better to be like Sarah? Was it better to be like Rocco, who followed Brody, even though he probably didn't always agree with everything Brody said and did?

Then Kal thought about the difference it made when DeeJay had stood up for her. And how Nikki had been forced to back down when Joey challenged her. She thought about how she'd stood up for herself when Brody had tried to tease her for not following along.

"It's not cool, Sarah," Kal said finally. "They shouldn't treat you like that."

"I know, but what can I do?" Sarah said.

"We can do something. We can teach Nikki a freakin' lesson," Kal said.

# 15 TOP OF THE EIGHTH INNING: ONE UP

As Kal walked through the school hallways, she felt like she was in a different world. Students were still staring at her, but the expressions on their faces were different. Instead of strange looks and prying eyes, there was nothing but smiles.

"Nice job, KaLeah!" said a group of younger girls as they walked past.

Next, one of Kal's teammates from Atco Lumber walked by and high-fived her.

Then Kal saw Brody, Rocco and a few other Trail Boys walking down the hall in front of her.

"Heads up!" Brody yelled at a girl walking in the other direction.

SLAP! Brody slapped the student's books out of her hands onto the hallway floor. He kicked her books, and all the papers in her binders spilled all over the hallway.

Brody laughed hysterically.

"Heads up!" Brody shouted again.

SLAP! Brody did the same thing to a boy walking past.

Kal shook her head and made a point of avoiding Brody.

She hurried down the hall to where Sarah was waiting at her locker.

"Are you ready to do this?" Kal asked.

"I don't know, Kal. I'm starting to think this isn't such a good idea," Sarah said.

"Do you want them to stop picking on you or not?" Kal asked.

"Well, yeah. But what if it just makes things worse?" Sarah asked.

"Sarah, it can't get much worse," Kal pointed out. "I've already talked to Joey," she continued. "He's into it. A little too much. I hope he doesn't screw this up; it has to look real."

"All right, let's do it," Sarah said.

Kal gave Sarah her phone. "Here, text Nikki's number to Joey. Everything is all set up."

Sarah took the phone and started texting. She handed the phone back to Kal.

Moments later a text buzzed Kal's phone.

"What does it say?" Sarah asked.

"Joey sent me what he just texted to Nikki. Here, see for yourself."

"You have his number!?"

"Just read the text, Sarah"

Sarah read the text:

Hi Nikki, it's Joey. I'm really sorry for what I posted on your Instagram. I actually really like you, but Kal is my friend and I had to stick up for her, IDK you were joking. Want to make it up to you. Come visit me at my ball game after school.

"Nikki is totally going to think he's going to ask her out," Sarah said.

"Yup," Kal said, smiling.

"Kal, that's mean," Sarah said.

"C'mon, Sarah, she deserves it!" Kal snapped back.

"Here she comes," Sarah whispered.

Nikki, Jenny and Marcy arrived at their lockers and started laughing at Sarah.

"How was the game, Sarah?" Nikki asked through her laughter.

"Very funny, guys," Sarah said.

"What are you staring at, Kal?" Nikki asked.

"Not much," Kal said.

"Whatever," Nikki said.

When Nikki opened her locker, her phone began to buzz. Nikki grabbed it to check her messages.

Kal watched as Nikki read the text. Nikki kissed the phone and then held it close to her chest. She turned around, her face beaming with excitement. "Girls, I think Joey is going to ask me out."

"What? Joey Neufeld?" Jenny shrieked.

"When?" Marcy added.

"Right now, I think. He wants to meet me at his ball game! Here, read this." Nikki handed her phone to show Marcy, Jenny and Sarah and started applying lip gloss.

"Wow, you're so lucky," Sarah said.

"Him posting that on my Instagram was just his way of getting my attention, I guess," Nikki said.

"Winking emoji! Wow, this is really happening. Are you ready?" Marcy asked.

Nikki took a deep breath and checked her reflection in the mirror in her locker. She grabbed her books and slammed the door shut.

"Okay, okay. Let's go," Nikki gushed.

The Valley Girls made their way past Kal out the school doors. Sarah followed close behind.

Kal sprinted all the way to the ballpark and arrived there ahead of the Valley Girls. She spotted Joey sitting in the bleachers in his uniform. The place was filled with people wearing Trail colours, orange and black. More people were streaming in from all over to watch the Trail high school baseball game.

Kal ran up to Joey. "Hey. She'll be here any minute."

"Cool. You going to stay after and watch the game?"

"Uh, yeah, probably."

"Probably? I'm pitching. My curveball is so dirty now. Thanks to you, babe."

Joey smiled and Kal felt her face start flushing.

Nikki, Marcy, Jenny and Sarah entered the ballpark.

Kal moved a short distance away. She pulled out her phone and focused her camera on Joey.

Just then, Brody and Rocco walked into the field. Brody was holding a large pop can and he was spitting dark gobs of saliva into it.

Chewing tobacco. *Gross*, Kal thought.

"Hey, Joey, you want a chew? Rocco and I got some," Brody said.

Kal became nervous. Brody and Rocco could ruin the whole thing.

"Nah, I'm good, fellas," Joey said.

As Nikki approached, Brody said in a loud voice, "Hey, Collins, want some chew?!"

"Get lost, Brody," Nikki said.

*Yeah, get lost, Brody,* Kal wanted to shout. But she kept quiet.

"Hi, Joey," Nikki said nervously.

Several of the Trail Boys, including DeeJay, walked into the park at that moment. Kal adjusted her camera position to get a clear shot. *There are so many people here*, thought Kal. But it was too late to stop now. Kal began recording.

"Who are you?" Joey said.

"It's me, Nikki."

"Nikki who?" Joey asked.

Nikki's face turned bright red.

A group of older girls joined the crowd forming around Joey. One pretty girl with curly long, red hair put her arm on Joey's shoulder. *Who's that?* wondered Kal.

"Hey, give me a minute," Joey said to her casually.

"I'm just joking," Joey said, turning back to Nikki. "I know who you are."

Kal could see Nikki breathe a sigh of relief. "You're so funny, Joey. I got your text," Nikki said, smiling from ear to ear.

"Yeah, about that text. You can forget it."

Kal moved in closer, still recording.

"What?" Nikki said, her face turning red.

"It was a joke, Nikki. I don't like you. And I'd never ask you out. I already have a girlfriend."

Joey put his arm around the girl with curly hair. Kal tried to focus on recording.

The girl turned and laughed in Nikki's face. "Who's this toddler?" the girl asked.

Kal zoomed in on Marcy's and Jenny's faces. Then she focused on Nikki's face.

Nikki looked at all the faces staring at her. She turned and stared right at Kal and the camera.

On the screen, Kal saw the look of pure embarrassment on Nikki's face.

Everyone in the bleachers started laughing. Kal couldn't believe it, even Marcy and Jenny started laughing, and they were supposed to be Nikki's friends.

Nikki turned to run away but she smashed right into Brody.

*Splash!* Dark gobs of chewing tobacco saliva spilled from the pop can he was holding all over Nikki.

"Watch it, Collins!"

Nikki was covered in dark gooey spit. It dripped down the front of her shirt onto her jeans. The bleachers erupted even louder with laughter.

Nikki stumbled and fell to the ground.

She got up and sprinted out of the park.

Kal stopped filming.

Sarah walked up beside Kal.

"Oh my gosh, that was like, really, really bad."

"The worst. It was the worst," Kal said quietly. She had not expected to embarrass Nikki that badly.

"Look at Marcy and Jenny," Sarah said.

Kal and Sarah watched as Marcy and Jenny quietly disappeared into the crowd.

Joey walked up to Kal.

"Kal, you got her real bad. That must've felt good after what she posted about you," Joey said.

Kal handed the phone to Sarah. Sarah looked over the footage.

"By the way, that's not really my girlfriend. It was all part of the act. Worked well, hey?" Joey said.

"It worked great," Kal said. A part of her was relieved that the girl wasn't anything special to Joey.

"So, you going to watch me play?" Joey asked.

Kal suddenly felt her face grow hot and her armpits begin to perspire.

Kal's mind was racing. Why was Joey still talking to her? He had a baseball game to play, and why was it so important that she watch him play? And why was he staring at her the same way he had when they were alone at the park? For a moment, she pictured Joey as her boyfriend. The thought made Kal's heart flutter. *What would people say?*

"Kal?"

"Of course, um, I'll be right back." Part of Kal wanted to just sit in the bleachers and enjoy her victory over the Valley Girls. She also didn't want to miss Joey's game. But the joke on Nikki had gone too far.

"Have you posted the video yet?" Sarah asked.

"No, not yet," Kal said.

Kal opened the Instagram app.

Kal felt terrible. She'd wanted to teach Nikki a lesson, and she did. But she couldn't get Nikki's look of horror out of her mind. She closed the Instagram app. Kal sprinted out the park in the direction she saw Nikki run.

"Where are you going?" Sarah shouted after her.

Kal just kept running.

# 16 BOTTOM OF THE EIGHTH INNING: NEW BEGINNINGS

Kal sprinted through the streets.

Kal could hear trumpet blasts from the baseball field in the distance. More people were flooding through the streets toward the ballpark as she ran in the opposite direction. Kal didn't know how or where she was going to find Nikki, but she had to. Kal jogged into a parking lot. No sign of Nikki anywhere.

Kal walked past a few cars, toward the back of the parking lot. She spotted Nikki sitting on the curb behind a large truck. Nikki was sobbing.

Kal walked up to Nikki and stood over top of her. Nikki was a mess. Her shirt and her jeans were stained and her face was covered in tears.

"Leave me alone," Nikki snapped at her.

"Hurts, doesn't it?" Kal said.

"I hate you," Nikki said.

Kal sat down beside Nikki. "I'm not going to post the video, Nikki."

Nikki turned to look at Kal. "Yeah, right."

"Seriously, I'm not going to," Kal said.

"Why wouldn't you?" Nikki asked.

"Because that's what you would have done to me. To Sarah, and to everyone else," Kal said.

"Why should I believe you when you say you're not going to?" Nikki said.

"You don't have to. I won't. But if you post anything else about me or Sarah or anyone else, the deal is off," Kal said.

"You put Joey up to that. He embarrassed me in front of everyone," Nikki said.

"That's exactly what you, Marcy and Jenny do to everyone," Kal said.

"Marcy and Jenny. Those bitches laughed at me just like everyone else," Nikki snorted.

"Yeah, they did. They were probably trying to save face. No one likes being teased or embarrassed," Kal said.

"I hate Brody. Did you tell him to do that to me?" Nikki asked.

"I can't stand Brody, either. I had nothing to do with that," Kal said.

"Someone should do something to him," Nikki said after a long time.

"I threw a plum at his head the other day," Kal said smiling.

"Nice!" Nikki said.

"Yeah, missed though," Kal said.

"It's the thought that counts," Nikki said, managing a laugh.

"Yeah," Kal agreed.

The two girls sat in silence for a moment.

"You know, I didn't mean all that stuff I said and posted about you," Nikki said.

"Why did you do it, then?" Kal asked.

"I don't know. You were new and different and getting a lot of attention. I didn't like that you were better than me in softball. I don't know; I thought it was funny. I'm sorry," Nikki said.

"I'm sorry for getting Joey to embarrass you like that. I just wanted to get back at you," Kal said.

"I guess I deserved some of that," Nikki said.

"You sure did." Kal thought about the racist teasing the Valley Girls dished out to her and Sarah. They might not have meant it, but it hurt.

"Not just from what you did to me," Kal added, "but how you, Marcy and Jenny treat Sarah. She showed me everything on Instagram, and the group texts, and she was super upset about that prank you pulled on her with the fake game."

"She never says anything; I guess we always thought she was laughing along with us," Nikki said.

"Yeah, no. She's totally not," Kal said.

"I guess we are pretty mean to her," Nikki said.

"Yeah. You girls are real bitches to everyone. Maybe someone should throw a plum at your head," Kal said.

"Oh, or chocolate pudding? Like you're not so innocent," Nikki said.

"How do you like a celery stick covered in cream cheese in your hair?" Kal said, smiling.

"Good point."

They both laughed. Nikki looked thoughtful. "Well, at least Joey was just joking about what he said about me. Maybe I still have a chance with him."

"I don't know about that," said Kal, smiling to herself.

"But you said you put him up to it."

"Yeah, but I didn't tell him to say all that. That was extra."

"Oh."

"Yeah, I'd back off if I were you."

"Why? So you can date him?"

"Me?"

"Yeah, you."

"We're just friends."

"Sure, Kal."

★★★

On Friday afternoon, Kal and Sarah sat in the cafeteria eating their lunches. They were surprised when Nikki led Jenny and Marcy to sit at their table.

"Hey, Kal, you want some of this celery stick? It's got cream cheese in it," Nikki joked as they dug into their lunches.

Sarah stopped chewing her sandwich and looked at Kal, expecting her to react.

Kal laughed and took a bite of her sandwich.

"Did I miss something?" Sarah asked.

Kal made eye contact with Nikki. She didn't hate her anymore. But she certainly didn't consider her as a friend.

Brody and Rocco walked by.

"Hey, you girls got a toonie I can bum off ya?" Brody asked.

"Beat it, Brody," Nikki snapped.

"Kal?" Brody asked.

"Go kick rocks, Brody," Kal said.

Nikki high-fived Kal.

"We'll see who is laughing when we kick Atco Lumber's ass this weekend at Silver City Days tournament," Brody said. He and Rocco walked away to ask other students for money.

Sarah put her sandwich down. "Okay, you two, now this is just getting weird."

"Totally," Marcy added.

"Are you two, like, besties now?" Jenny laughed.

Both Kal and Nikki shrugged their shoulders. It was weird — a week ago, Nikki was her worst enemy. *This was better.* Kal was glad she didn't post the video.

"Brody smells," Sarah said.

Nikki shot a quick glance at Sarah, then started laughing. The girls all joined in.

Kal thought she'd never seen Sarah look so happy.

DeeJay came to stand behind Kal. Kal noticed that Sarah's face turned bright red when DeeJay gave her a big smile.

"Hi, Sarah. Kal, I need to talk to you real quick," said DeeJay. He led Kal a little way from the table.

"Do you think Brody is a better player than me?" DeeJay asked. He seemed uneasy.

Kal didn't know how to answer.

"Really, Kal?" DeeJay snapped.

"Whoa easy, you're better. That's obvious. What's up?" Kal asked.

"Brody embarrassed me last year in front of everyone during Silver City Days," DeeJay said.

"What happened?" Kal asked.

"It doesn't matter now. All that matters is that this year, we have to win. So bring your A game; I'm not losing to Big O Tire this year."

"This might be a stupid question, but what are Silver City Days?" Kal asked as they sat down at the table with the other girls.

"Really, Kal?" Nikki said.

"I'm new, remember."

"Silver City Days is like the town's anniversary celebration. There's a parade, a fair, fireworks and amusement park rides going on downtown. It's, like, the best weekend of the year," Nikki said.

"And it's the biggest house league tournament of

the year," DeeJay said. He nudged Kal, and she realized how important it was to DeeJay that their team beat Brody's.

"You girls should come watch us play." DeeJay flashed another smile at Sarah before he walked away.

"I saw that, Sarah," Kal said, smiling.

"Me too," Marcy said.

"I saw it, too," Jenny said.

"Everyone saw that, Sarah," Nikki added.

"Saw what?" Sarah said as her face turned bright red again.

"I hope you guys beat Brody's team this year, Kal. Last year, DeeJay's team lost in the final. Brody was all over him for crying to his dad about it," Nikki said.

Kal nodded. She thought that it must be hard to live up to having a dad who was such a tough coach. And it wasn't just DeeJay who had something to prove to Coach Smith.

More than anything, she wanted to show up Brody and prove herself to Coach Smith.

Nikki smirked at Kal.

"Kal, you think Joey is going to be there? I hope he is. Maybe I can . . ."

"Hey, want some pudding, Nikki?" Kal said, threatening to flick some off her spoon in Nikki's direction.

"Don't you dare!" Nikki said, brandishing a celery stick.

# 17 TOP OF THE NINTH INNING: SILVER CITY DAYS

After school, Kal, Nikki and Sarah headed to the fair-grounds for Silver City Days. They ate cotton candy, joined in watermelon-eating contests and went on the Ferris wheel. Marcy and Jenny joined them later in the afternoon, and the five girls decided to visit the haunted house.

As they walked along the dark corridors, plastic spiders dropped from the ceiling.

Sarah shrieked.

"C'mon, Sarah, that wasn't even scary," Kal said.

"I hate spiders," Sarah said.

They turned a corner and someone jumped out at them in the shadows.

"Heads up!" The figure in the shadows sprayed them with a water gun, soaking them from head to toe.

It was Brody. He ran out of the haunted house, laughing his head off.

Nikki fumed. "I hate that Brody."

★★★

By the time Kal got home, it was almost dark. Except for what Brody did, the day had been one of the best days she'd had since moving to Trail.

Her dad met her at the door with an upset look on his face.

"What's up, Dad?" Kal asked.

"I just got off the phone with Coach Smith."

"Yeah?" Kal said.

"He said some of the parents in the league were talking. They don't think you should return to play on the team. They think it might be too dangerous for you, after you got hit so hard by that pitch."

Kal's stomach tied in knots. "Does the rest of the team know about this?" she asked.

"No, he wanted to keep this between us."

"Is Coach Smith kicking me off the team?"

"No, he can't do that," her dad said. "But he wanted me to talk to you about it."

"Well, there's nothing to talk about. I'm playing. I don't care what anyone says." Kal stormed into the house.

That evening Kal sat in her bed. Who were these parents who didn't think she should play baseball? Kal knew one of them must be Sam's dad, because she had taken Sam's position.

The thought of people thinking she shouldn't be

playing baseball bothered Kal. It really bothered her because it was just because she was a girl. Kal got up from her bed and got the picture of her mother from her dresser. Her mother always encouraged her to play baseball. She told Kal that she couldn't let fear stop her from being her best. Kal realized that it wasn't just her fear, but other people's fear that might stand in her way.

Kal thought of the newspaper clippings Joey had shown her at Trail Memorial Centre. She wondered if people had told Kelly Craig she couldn't play. Did boys hit her with pitches? Kal decided that Kelly probably went through the same thing. But she played her best anyway and she ended up in the Hall of Fame.

Trail was the Home of Champions. Just a little while ago, Kal was a stranger, the new kid and the only black girl in town. She'd felt alone. Now, thanks to baseball, she had friends and teammates who stood up for her. Trail was becoming her home.

*Knock, knock.* Kal's dad opened the door slowly.

"Honey, I just want you to know that I support you one hundred percent. I called Coach Smith back and thanked him for his concern. But I said you're playing."

"Thanks, Dad," Kal said.

"Get some sleep — big game tomorrow," her dad said, closing the door behind him.

Kal jumped back into her bed and turned out the lights.

She closed her eyes and pictured herself playing the best game of baseball she had ever played.

★★★

When Kal arrived at the ballpark, she was shocked at the number of people. It looked like the entire town of Trail was there. Kal saw most of her classmates had come to watch their game. Nikki, Sarah, Jenny and Marcy had painted their faces the Atco Lumber team colours. This tournament was a way bigger deal than she had imagined.

Kal walked into the dugout. DeeJay and the rest of her teammates greeted her with smiles and pats on the back.

The moment was interrupted by a loud voice.

"We wouldn't want anyone getting hurt today, Coach! Do the right thing, Coach! Do the right thing!" Mr. Davis yelled into the dugout.

Kal scanned the faces of some of the parents in the stands, many of them were nodding in agreement.

"Let's do this, Kal!" DeeJay shouted.

Coach Smith stood behind DeeJay with his arms crossed. He looked at Kal square in the eyes.

Kal removed Trapper from her backpack.

"I'm ready to play, Coach," Kal said firmly.

Coach Smith stood without saying a word. He scratched his head and turned away. "Sam, get suited up," he said over his shoulder.

DeeJay gave his dad a shocked look. "Seriously, Dad?"

"Get out there, son! Worry about yourself," Coach Smith shouted back.

Kal grabbed her catcher's gear and began suiting up anyway. She fought back the tears in her eyes and acted like the Coach's decision didn't bother her. But it cut deep like a knife.

"Play ball!" the umpire yelled.

*Roar!* The crowd erupted in applause. There were so many people at the ballpark, there weren't enough seats to fit them all. There were people standing on the fence, and some people had set up lawn chairs along the grassy banks beside the field. There were people everywhere Kal looked.

*CLANG! CLANG!* Fans held up cowbells and rang them as the players took the field.

Atco Lumber took bat first and Rocco struck out the first three batters. Kal could see he was on his game.

First up to bat for Big O Tire in the bottom of the first inning was Rocco.

DeeJay wound up and fired his first pitch.

*CRANK!* Rocco launched the ball deep to left field. Kal couldn't believe that such a skinny boy could have so much power in his swing.

Kal stood and watched as the ball sailed over the left field fence. Rocco had hit a home run.

Rocco rounded the bases clapping his hands.

Kal looked at the scoreboard: BIG O TIRE 1 — ATCO LUMBER 0.

"Settle down, DeeJay!" Coach Smith shouted from the dugout.

DeeJay walked the next batter with four wild pitches.

"Relax, DeeJay," Kal shouted from the dugout.

DeeJay nodded at Kal. He smiled and she could see his shoulders relax. He struck out the next batter with three blistering fastballs.

Coach Smith and Kal exchanged looks.

"He listens to you," Coach Smith said.

"We're teammates," Kal said.

Coach Smith nodded.

Next up was Brody.

"BOO!" Nikki, Sarah, Marcy and Jenny yelled from the stands as Brody stepped into the batter's box, Hugo in his hand.

DeeJay wound up and fired a pitch. Brody swung.

*Clink! Smack!* Brody fouled the ball straight back and it hit Sam right in his throwing hand.

"Ouch! Ouch! Ouch!" Sam jumped out from behind the plate, waving his hand frantically. Sam's dad ran onto the field.

"Someone get some ice!" Mr. Davis shouted.

Kal's dad rushed onto the field.

"Let me take a look at it," Kal's dad said as he examined Sam's hand. "It might be broken."

"How could this happen? Sam, how do you feel? Can you play?" Mr. Davis asked.

Kal's dad turned to Mr. Davis. "Baseball is a dangerous game; these types of things can happen to anyone," he said. "You better get him some X-rays. Hang in there, Sam."

Mr. Davis helped Sam off the field.

Coach Smith walked back to the dugout.

"Sam's hand looks broken. He's off to the hospital to get it looked at."

Kal remained silent. She hoped Sam was okay. But more than that, she hoped Coach Smith would let her play.

"You ready?" Coach Smith asked, turning to face Kal

"Sure am, Coach!" Kal shouted. She hadn't meant to shout, but she couldn't contain herself.

Coach Smith smiled. "Get in there."

Kal jogged onto the field and ran straight to the mound to DeeJay.

"Is that your friend Sarah in the stands?" he asked.

"Yeah, why?"

"No reason."

Kal could tell there was something more. But now wasn't the time. DeeJay's mind seemed to be focused on everything except on his pitching.

"You need to focus, DeeJay," she said.

"I'm losing it for us, Kal. I'm glad you're in, but I don't know if I can do this."

"You're the best pitcher in house league. You just need to settle down, DeeJay."

"I know. I can't believe Rocco took me deep," DeeJay said, frustrated.

"It's only the first inning. We'll get it back," Kal said.

The two touched gloves and Kal took her position behind the plate.

"Play ball!" the umpire shouted.

Brody stepped into the batter's box. He scowled at Kal and DeeJay.

Kal called for the fastball. DeeJay delivered the pitch.

"Strike two!"

DeeJay fired another pitch.

*CRANK!* Brody hit the ball high and deep into right field.

The ball sailed over the fence into the forest behind the park for a home run.

Brody rounded the bases pointing into the stands.

Big O Tire 3 − Atco Lumber 0

Kal could see that DeeJay was losing his cool. She ran to the mound and shoved Trapper into DeeJay's chest to get his attention. "Hey! We'll get it back!"

Kal's encouragement worked. DeeJay struck out the next two batters.

In the dugout, DeeJay was upset that he'd given up the three runs in the first inning.

"You've got to focus, man. We're in this together. Forget about last year!" Kal shouted.

DeeJay took a drink from his water bottle and poured the rest over his head.

"I just don't have my best stuff today."

"C'mon. You're the best player out here. Let's go!"

# 18 BOTTOM OF THE NINTH INNING: HEART OF A CHAMPION

Rocco was throwing harder than Kal had ever seen him throw.

Against the first batter, Rocco lost control of the pitch and hit the batter in the thigh. The batter limped to first base.

Kal was up next. She stepped into the batter's box.

Rocco wound up and fired a curveball. Kal had been expecting a fastball. She swung and missed badly.

"Strike one."

Rocco wound and threw another curveball. This time, Kal was ready for it.

*CRANK!* Kal hit the ball sharply and it went deep to centre field.

"Get out of here, ball," Kal said as she ran toward first base.

*SMASH!* The ball slammed into the scoreboard out in centre field. It was a home run.

Kal held her fist high in the air as she rounded the bases. It was the first home run she'd hit in Trail and it was a two-run blast!

The scoreboard read BIG O TIRE 3 – ATCO LUMBER 2.

*DING! DING!* The cowbells rang loud as she rounded the bases. She could see Marcy, Jenny, Nikki and Sarah high-fiving each other.

"Well, I'll be . . . atta girl!" Coach Smith said.

"Your turn!" Kal shouted at DeeJay.

The home run seemed to rattle Rocco a little.

DeeJay stepped up to the plate.

He swung at the first pitch Rocco threw and launched the ball over the scoreboard in centre field for another home run.

*ROAR!* The crowd cheered even louder as DeeJay rounded the bases.

"That's the way! We're right back in it!" Coach Smith shouted. He smiled and clapped his hands. "All right, let's keep it going!" Coach Smith shouted to the team.

Rocco got the next three batters to ground out to end the inning with the score tied: 3–3.

The rest of the game turned into a pitching duel between Rocco and DeeJay. Both pitchers were pitching perfectly, striking out batters and not allowing anyone to get on base. At the end of the seventh inning, the two teams were still tied.

They were going into extra innings.

Kal played well in the field. On one play, she fielded a bunt with her bare hand and threw the runner out at first base. But the teams were so evenly matched that at the top of the ninth inning, the game was still tied.

Rocco was getting tired; his fastballs weren't moving with as much speed as they had been earlier in the game. But he struck out the first Atco Lumber batter.

The next batter hit a soft ground ball right back to Rocco. Rocco fielded the ball and threw the runner out at first base. Two out.

Kal stepped up to bat.

When the coach for Big O Tire called timeout, Kal knew what was happening. The coach signalled for Brody to come in from left field.

Brody took the mound and began warming up.

Kal's mind raced. Would Brody try to hit her again?

"Play ball!" the umpire shouted.

Kal stepped into the batter's box.

The first pitch Brody threw came in high and right at Kal's head. She ducked out of the way and landed on her butt in the dirt.

"Chin music," Brody snorted.

"BOO!" the crowd shouted.

Kal got up and dusted herself off. She picked up some dirt and rubbed it in her palms.

The next pitch from Brody came in and Kal backed away from the plate.

"Strike one!"

Kal tried to focus. She kept thinking he would hit her again. But she stepped back into the batter's box. Brody fired another pitch.

Kal backed out and just watched. *Smack!* The ball hit the catcher's glove on the outside corner of the plate.

"Strike two!"

With two strikes against her, and her team depending on her, Kal narrowed her focus.

Brody fired again.

This time Kal didn't back away. She stood her ground and swung smoothly.

The ball shot away from her bat, going sharply up the middle. *Crack!* It hit Brody in the knee.

Kal sprinted to first and made it there without a throw. The ball had bounced off Brody's leg and no infielder was able to make a play to throw Kal out.

Brody rubbed his knee and glared at Kal.

When DeeJay stepped up to the plate, Kal could tell that he was determined to beat Brody.

Brody threw a fastball.

*CRANK!* DeeJay hit the ball so hard that before Kal could blink, it ricocheted off the left field fence.

"Yes!" Kal shouted as she rounded the bases and touched home plate.

*ROAR!* The crowd erupted in a thunderous applause. DeeJay cruised into third base.

Big O Tire 3 – Atco Lumber 4.

As Atco Lumber celebrated in the dugout, Brody got out of the inning by striking out the next batter.

Atco Lumber was just three outs away from victory.

DeeJay started off the bottom of the ninth inning pitching strong. He struck out the first batter. Then Brody stepped up to the plate.

DeeJay wound up and threw the pitch.

*CRACK!* Brody hit a line drive into centre field for a base hit.

Kal watched as Brody tried to pump his teammates up at first base. She could tell he wanted to win more than anything.

And Brody's hit seemed to have rattled DeeJay. He walked the next batter and Brody moved on to second base.

DeeJay's next pitch hit the next batter in the leg to load the bases.

"Time!" Coach Smith yelled.

A nervous hush went over the crowd. All Big O Tire needed was a base hit for the lead. Atco Lumber needed a double play to get three Big O Tire players out before they could score a run.

Coach Smith called the outfield to move in closer and advised the same to the infielders.

"Kal, be ready for a throw to home plate. We have to protect home plate if they put the ball in play. We can't let them get that run," Coach Smith said.

Kal stared down at third base at Brody. "I'll be ready," she said.

The Big O Tire batter stepped to the plate.

"Let's go, DeeJay," Kal shouted.

DeeJay wound up and threw a fastball.

*CRANK!* The Big O Tire batter hit a line drive into the ground toward first base.

The Atco Lumber first baseman snagged the ball and stepped on first base for the first out.

Brody had started running as soon as the ball was hit. Kal could see him bearing down on her out of the corner of her eye.

Kal jumped up, flipped off her mask and stood in Brody's path, blocking the plate.

"He's coming home!" Kal shouted.

The first basemen bobbled the ball.

"Throw home!" Kal shouted again.

Brody was just a few strides away and Kal could hear him grunting as he charged toward her.

The first basemen fired the ball back to Kal.

Kal caught the ball and turned. She saw Brody running full speed straight at her.

Kal put both hands on Trapper to secure the ball for the tag. She braced herself for the impact.

*THUD!* Brody ran right into Kal and knocked her over.

Kal landed flat on her back behind home plate. Her whole body hurt from the collision, but she didn't care. She could feel the ball still in her glove.

Her teammates gathered around her.

A hush fell over the crowd.

Kal sat up and held her glove in the air to show the

umpire the baseball in her glove.

"You're out!" the umpire shouted at Brody.

*ROAR!* The crowd erupted in a thunderous cheer.

*DING DING DING!* Cowbells rang throughout the field.

Kal's dad raised his hands in the air in celebration.

Sarah, Nikki, Marcy and Jenny jumped up and down, hugging each other and cheering.

Kal's teammates jumped on top of her.

Coach Smith clapped his hands.

"Hey, don't kill my catcher," he laughed. "I need her for the next game!"

Beneath the pile of players, Kal laughed and cheered with her teammates.

One by one, Kal's teammates climbed off her. When she finally sat up, Coach Smith smiled and held out his hand to help her up to her feet.

As soon as Kal was standing, the crowd erupted in applause. Kal scanned the crowd for her dad. She found him in the stands, a proud smile splitting his face. For a moment, sadness swept over Kal. She wished her mom was alive to see this. Kal took comfort as she imagined how happy and proud her mother would have been of her.

"Hell of a play, Kal," Rocco said, running to the dugout.

"Thanks, Rocco," Kal replied.

Brody walked by and patted Kal on the back. He

kept walking past without stopping. Kal could tell he was upset.

"Nice play," Brody said over his shoulder.

Kal winked at the Valley Girls. To her surprise, she saw Joey in the stands a few rows below them.

Joey smiled at her, before putting his fingers in his mouth and whistling loudly. Kal smiled back so wide she thought her face would split.

*How could this day get any better?* Kal wondered.

Coach Smith placed his arm around Kal's shoulders.

"You're a natural, Kal. You ever think about playing for the Trail All-Star team?" he said.